AMISH INN MYSTERIES™

To Honor *and* Betray

Rachael O. Phillips

Annie's®

AnniesFiction.com

Books in the Amish Inn Mysteries series

Secrets of the Amish Diary
Plain Deception
Simple Lies
Murder Simply Played
To Love and to Vanish
Law & Old Order
A Silent Betrayal
Humble Pies and White Lies
Deceptive Hearts
Stolen Past
Grave Inheritance
Homespun Homicide
Broken Melody
Horse and Burglary
A Fatal Harvest
A Simple Deduction
The Hound and the Fury
Unhappy Returns
Skating the Law
Book Clubbed
Farmed Robbery
Scene of the Chime
Amish and Old Lace
To Honor and Betray

To Honor and Betray

Library of Congress-in-Publication Data
To Honor and Betray / by Rachael O. Phillips
p. cm.
I. Title
2018936892

AnniesFiction.com
(800) 282-6643
Amish Inn Mysteries™
Series Creator: Shari Lohner
Series Editor: Jane Haertel
Cover Illustrator: Kelley McMorris

10 11 12 13 14 | Printed in China | 9 8 7 6 5 4 3

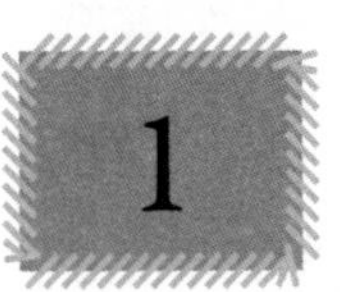

"Jackson wants to keep the wedding simple. 'It's not a celebrity bash, for goodness' sake.'" Liz Eckardt mimicked her fiancé, then slumped into a chair in dismay. "He thinks I'm obsessing over details, but—"

"What does *he* know about weddings?" Sadie Schwarzentruber snorted. The huge knitted sunflowers on her hat flapped as she attacked blue fabric with her scissors. "He's a smart mayor, but he's a man. Men flunk Wedding 101 every time."

Liz smiled. "I thought because he's run so many festivals that he'd understand what goes into planning even a 'simple' wedding."

Mary Ann Berne, Sadie's partner in the Sew Welcome Shop, which was located in Liz's bed-and-breakfast, the Olde Mansion Inn, threaded a needle and tied a firm knot at the end. "The Y chromosomes do erase any sense of reality when it comes to nuptials."

Terrence Pike, a textiles professor and also a guest at the inn, added a few stitches to the seam he was working on.

"What's the matter, Terry?" Sadie brought him more quilt blocks and clapped him on the shoulder hard enough to make his graying ponytail sway. "Feeling outnumbered?"

Liz winced. *Terrence, not Terry.* Sometimes Sadie overstepped in treating Liz's guests like family.

However, the man didn't seem to mind. "My four sisters still treat me like their baby brother. I can take anything you ladies dish out."

"Oh, yeah?" Sadie waved her scissors at Terrence.

"Yeah." He waved his scissors back.

Amid the laughter, Mary Ann, ever the committee chairwoman, tried to steer them back to task. "No bloodshed, please. We want to finish Liz's quilt well before her wedding."

Everyone made an effort to refocus. Another guest, Vanessa Leighton, a business supplies sales executive, was improving her rudimentary sewing skills as Miriam, Liz's beloved Amish cousin, helped her. Now halfway through the evening, Vanessa had managed to stitch a straight line. Once.

Wedding talk mingled with every other conversation topic.

"Remember, we're all here to help you." Opal Ringenberg said. Her quiet words reassured Liz.

Her dear friends from the Material Girls quilting group were not only piecing this lovely blue, cream, and green Double Wedding Ring quilt for her and Jackson, but they were also shouldering responsibilities in many other areas. Mary Ann had assumed the position of wedding coordinator, with Sadie as assistant. Opal was overseeing decorations. Naomi Mason, who owned Sweet Everything, the bakery next door, would create a memorable cake. Twentysomething nurse Caitlyn Ross would help Liz with her hair and makeup on the day.

And Kiera Williams, her former part-time gardener at the Olde Mansion Inn, had been taking singing lessons in college. During her last visit to Pleasant Creek, Kiera had wowed everyone with her lovely voice. She'd agreed to sing at the wedding.

That reminds me . . .

"Do you want to hear a song I'm considering?" Liz paused in pressing one of the quilt blocks and pulled out her phone.

"Oh, good. You finally found one you liked?" Naomi stuck her needle into a pincushion. The others clamored to hear.

"Yes. It's called, 'Love, You Are My Friend.'"

"May I hear it too?" a deep voice said.

Liz turned to see the gleam in Jackson's hazel eyes and his irresistible grin.

"Thought I'd drop by for refreshment time." He kissed her lightly.

"Perfect timing," Caitlyn said. "Play the song, Liz."

Jackson laughed. "I'd like to hear it too." He turned back to Liz. "This is a new one, right?"

"Yes, I heard it on the radio, and I can't get it out of my head." Liz picked up her phone and summoned her playlist. "It's rather haunting, but beautiful. See what you think."

Acoustic guitar chords filled the room, and silence fell as a rich male voice sang:

I run from love—love is too thorny, not worth a rose that will never last.

I run from love because love ran from me—I can't forget the pain of my past.

Yet Love sent me to those who cared,

Heard my crying and they dared

To take me home. Make me their own.

Love, you were my friend.

So I have to believe that someday I'll stop running.

I have to believe that someday I'll stop shunning

The love sent by Love who wants to take me home,

Make me her own forever,

Though even if you'd stay, I'd sprint the other way . . .

Love, you'll be my friend.

Love, you'll be my friend.

"'Love, you'll be my friend.' I adore that line." Caitlyn had a hand on her chest and a rapturous expression on her face. "I may have that song at my wedding someday."

"Cool song," Terrence agreed. "Guy can play that guitar."

Others chimed in approval, but Mary Ann cocked her head. "I like it too, but what does the groom say?"

Jackson spread his hands in a fake helpless gesture. "As if what I say matters."

Oh, no you don't. No smiling and caving just because I like it. Liz eyed him. "You know it does."

Jackson seemed to be considering. "I love the thoughtful lyrics and the tune. And I agree, Caitlyn, 'Love, you'll be my friend' says it all. But the song's a little sad. It sounds like this guy hasn't found love again after a disappointment." His arm tightened around Liz. "We have."

"Yes, we have." She hugged his lean waist. "We don't have to use that song. I'm not sure why it moves me. I keep waiting for Trey Edmond to sing another verse about finally having found love that will last."

"Trey Edmond writes most of his own songs, doesn't he?" Naomi shoved her traditional gooey sweet rolls into the microwave.

"I think so. This one's brand new. But it sounds so familiar." Liz frowned. "Maybe I'm mixing up two songs."

"Many modern songs sound similar." Opal didn't exactly sniff, but her pursed mouth expressed her opinion of current hits. "Though this one's prettier than the yelling I hear on the radio."

"You're right." Vanessa shook her head, smiling. "The songs my granddaughters play all sound alike to me."

Caitlyn's eyes widened. "You don't look old enough to have grandchildren."

Vanessa's blue eyes twinkled. "I certainly am. And I like my music sweet and simple, just like that one."

The microwave's *ding* and the smell of cinnamon-laden sweet rolls interrupted the musical discussion.

As sunset occurred earlier every day, Miriam took her roll "to go" and left for her buggy, which was parked out front.

After her departure, a lively debate between oldies advocates and current-hit fans resumed until Sadie finished off the evening with a hip-swiveling Elvis impression of "Burning Love."

Beans, the perpetually comatose brown-and-white English bulldog Liz had inherited with her inn purchase, had been rudely awakened by the ruckus. He left his cherished rug in the inn's entry and howled along with Sadie's rendition.

Jackson tied the full garbage bag once everyone else had tidied up and were making their departures. "After I take out the trash, want to meet me at your bench and watch the stars come out?"

"Sure." Liz grinned at the prospect as they followed Mary Ann out Sew Welcome's entrance into the rotunda of Liz's inn.

Mary Ann locked the shop door. "Don't stay out late, children. Workday tomorrow."

A few minutes later, Jackson's smile warmed Liz as he joined her in what had been her favorite solitary spot on a bench surrounded by lilac bushes in the inn's backyard and was now her favorite spot to share with him. Liz's shoulders relaxed against Jackson's arm, and he drew her close as cicadas performed their free nightly concert, accompanied by the lap of Jaynes Lake waves.

After a few minutes of silence, Jackson ventured, "We can have 'Love, You Are My Friend' at the wedding, if you want."

"Oh, Jackson, it's not essential. Our wedding's important, but not as important as our marriage."

"Glad we have that straight." He hugged her again.

"I've seen too many bridezillas who believe the universe turns around her 'special day.'" Liz shuddered. "And they spend all their money trying to make it happen."

"Thank goodness you're not that woman."

Together, they'd kept wedding expenses reasonable. But the cost of remodeling part of the inn's third floor into a home office and man cave for Jackson—Liz had decided against adding another guest suite since she really had as much business as she could handle most of the time—had increased substantially when the contractor found roof leaks. And Jackson's house hadn't sold yet, though Steve was thinking of renting it. She was still overjoyed to have her adopted son living near her now that he had completed his time in the military.

Liz's thoughts fluttered uneasily around blown budgets until Jackson's voice drew them back to their wedding.

"Do you think we might add a few words to 'Love, You Are My Friend'? Something more positive and hopeful about love? Because I like the song too."

"Maybe." She *hmmed*. "We'll have to find a poet, though."

2

Geoffrey Teal, who arrived the next day, could have won the "Guest of the Year" award, if there was such a thing.

Tall and muscular, Geoffrey wore a well-trimmed brown beard and mustache that accentuated his strong jawline. He arrived on time and had even brought Liz a small, tasteful bouquet.

Speaking with a touch of a Southern accent, he said, "My mama always said I shouldn't come empty-handed to anyone's house."

He showed her a beautiful guitar. "I'm playing for several gigs around here over Labor Day weekend."

Liz took a photo of him and his guitar for the inn's scrapbook. "Perhaps I can come and hear you play at one of your events." For once, Pleasant Creek wasn't hosting a festival that would require her or Jackson's attention, a fact she appreciated during her wedding month.

"I'll be glad to play for you and your other guests." Geoffrey flashed his winning smile.

"Perhaps at coffee hour?" Maybe he'd let her put a brief video on her inn's website.

"Not today." He sounded truly regretful. "I have a gig tonight. Tomorrow?"

"Perfect." She'd invite Jackson, the Material Girls, and maybe the Pleasant Creek police chief, Stan Houghton, a longtime friend. Steve too—it would be a good excuse to see her adopted son, who had his own apartment now. "What's your favorite cookie?"

"All of them." Geoffrey chuckled. "But I am partial to macadamia-nut anything."

"You may have to fight my son for them." Liz grinned. "But I'll bake enough for you both."

Hammering echoed from the upper floors. Liz grimaced. "I forgot to tell you—carpenters are working in the attic. But they quit at five sharp, and they won't work over the long weekend."

"No problem," he said cheerfully. "I'll probably be out most of the time anyway."

After scratching Beans's ears, Geoffrey insisted on carrying his guitar, amp, and large leather bags upstairs himself.

Barring walk-in guests, she didn't expect others until Friday. With the wedding and remodeling to manage, she didn't mind the inn being less than full. That is, she didn't mind until the hammering made her recall her expense spreadsheets. If only that roof hadn't leaked!

Chill, Liz. Would she spend these next special weeks obsessing over events she couldn't control? Now that Geoffrey was settled, Liz walked across the rotunda to unlock the small apartment she soon would share with Jackson. After pouring herself raspberry tea, she took her late mother's old diary from a bedside stand and curled up on the sofa.

Smoothing its faded yellow cover unknotted Liz's neck muscles. Her mother, born Deborah Miller, had left the Amish faith and moved to Boston, where she'd changed her name to Abigail Byler. There, she met and married Liz's father, Mark Eckardt. Mark had died when Liz was a preschooler, and her memories of him were fleeting. But it had been this diary that brought Liz to Pleasant Creek, the little town she now called home and the place where she'd learned the secret of her mother's early life.

Since then, she'd been blessed beyond her wildest dreams. There were Jackson, the Material Girls, her mother's Amish family, who had welcomed her into their lives, and this beautiful inn. It was all a dream come true.

When she put everything into perspective, she knew that there was no point obsessing over small matters like money. She had everything she wanted or needed right there.

Liz headed for the kitchen to prepare for coffee hour. Today, it might consist of only Vanessa and Liz, as Terrence was teaching at a local college. But Liz would use her vintage china and arrange cookies on a pretty plate as if a famous person were visiting.

Because in her mind, every guest was a celebrity.

The next day's coffee hour, however, proved worthy of a photo op.

"That's the loveliest houseplant I've ever seen!" Naomi gaped at Geoffrey's newest hostess gift.

"Those red flowers are gorgeous." Mary Ann glanced toward the beaming musician. "A castor bean plant, you say?"

He nodded. "The tag says that with plenty of light, it'll grow amazingly."

"I'll leave this out for everyone to enjoy for a while, then put it in my quarters where there's a south-facing window." Liz, touching the plant's shiny, bronze-colored leaves, cast a grateful glance at her guest. "Thanks again, Geoffrey."

He tuned his guitar as Jackson, Steve, the Material Girls, Vanessa, and Chief Houghton brewed favorite coffees and teas. They filled crystal dessert plates with chocolate chip cookies and Liz's lemon poppy seed bread.

Despite Geoffrey's penchant for cookies, the poppy seed bread's taste halted his active fingers. "I don't cook, but I'll learn if you'll give me that recipe."

He wowed them with a guitar medley of current hits, ending with a beautifully performed ballad.

"You don't sing?" Mary Ann asked.

He shrugged. "Got a decent voice, but nothing great. I'd really rather play."

"You're very good," Jackson said. "I like your sound."

Liz had thought of asking Geoffrey if he'd come back to the inn and play for their wedding. In her mind, she heard that talented strumming behind Kiera's sweet voice singing "Love, You Are My Friend."

But before she could ask, he mentioned that he was booked that weekend. Answering the others' questions, the musician told them about his upcoming performances, including one on the last Saturday of September, their wedding date. Liz swallowed her disappointment.

"This is the best gig, though," Geoffrey added. "Hanging with friends, jamming. And eating poppy seed bread." Grinning, he popped a large piece into his mouth.

After the mini-concert, Vanessa, who had heard Liz was a transplanted Hoosier, asked how she'd come to Pleasant Creek. Jackson and Liz's friends filled her guests in on how the diary and baby quilt bequeathed to her by her late mother had prompted Liz to seek her unexpected Amish family in Indiana.

"Fascinating." Vanessa smoothed her short, highlighted hair. "I'm glad I met your cousin Miriam. I've always wanted to know more about the Amish, and Miriam is such a talented quilter."

Geoffrey said, "I heard you solve mysteries, Liz. Is that true?"

"You don't know the half," Sadie bragged, and told him and Vanessa all about Liz's exploits.

Trying to steer it elsewhere, Liz attempted to draw Steve into chatting with her guests. He talked awhile with Vanessa, whose son had been in the military, then shot the breeze with Caitlyn, who was closest to his age. But after that, Steve said little.

Vanessa rose to leave for dinner with a potential customer. Geoffrey was meeting with a musician friend soon.

"Loved your playing," Caitlyn enthused as Geoffrey passed her. "Maybe I'll bring friends to hear you this weekend."

"Awesome! Glad you enjoyed it." The musician carried his guitar up the stairs in the rotunda.

Mary Ann accosted Liz. "We should go shopping for your reception. Soon."

"I know." She'd thought the days before her wedding would drag. Nothing could be further from the truth.

"You'd better not let Mary Ann loose without you," Sadie advised.

Her partner frowned. "What's that supposed to mean?"

"Nothing." Sadie's angelic smile sent a twinge of uneasiness through Liz.

Nevertheless, she knew exactly what Sadie meant. Given free rein, Mary Ann would create a reception that would rival a White House gala.

That wasn't what she and Jackson had in mind. Liz said hastily, "Are you doing anything this evening?"

Mary Ann grabbed at the offer. "Tonight would work."

"Let's all go!" Sadie proposed. "You're off, aren't you, Caitlyn? Naomi, Opal—you can go, can't you?"

At their nods, Sadie clapped her hands. "Let's help Liz clean up, and then we'll take the van."

Teacups, mugs, and spoons were banished to the dishwasher, and crumbs were vacuumed as she and Jackson exchanged glances.

He whispered in her ear, "Stick up for yourself, Liz. Don't worry—the reception will turn out great. Call me when you get home."

She nodded and watched him leave—then realized the Material Girls were all watching her. Liz reminded herself that time would dispel all the small-town brouhaha, including her friends' over-the-top ideas.

Till then, she might as well enjoy being the center of attention.

Grabbing her bag, she grinned. "What are we waiting for? We've got the reception of the year to plan!"

Riding home in the loaded Sew Welcome van, which was affectionately called the Patchwork Bomb because of its garish paint job, Liz chided herself for worrying needlessly. Her friends' input had proved valuable, not intrusive—other than Sadie's insistence that all September weddings included sunflowers, which was exactly why Liz didn't choose them. Still, she couldn't escape the fear that Sadie would make them all floppy hats like hers. Thankfully, Liz didn't have to play bridezilla, as Mary Ann and their friends reminded Sadie it was Liz's wedding.

The lanterns, strings of lights, silk flowers and ribbons in peach, cream, and yellow, and yards of creamy tulle were exactly what she'd wanted.

Carrying bags and boxes, her friends followed Liz through the inn's front door as she flipped on the rotunda lights.

Beans barely flicked a whisker.

"Some watchdog you are," Liz scolded, though his typical comatose state assured her all was well.

Sadie defended him. "Poor Beans was looking peaked yesterday. He needs his sleep."

"Uh-huh." Suddenly weary, Liz was in no mood to discuss Beans's health, which Sadie could do for hours. Setting down her purchases, Liz fumbled keys from her bag and headed for the door of her quarters.

Then halted in her tracks.

The door was still closed. But its hardware was scratched and bent. Someone had tried to break in.

Jackson arrived at the inn before the police. The Material Girls, who had circled Liz, parted so he could join them.

"Nothing like a little pre-wedding excitement." Despite the attempt at humor, Jackson's tone held none of its usual lightness.

Chief Stan Houghton and Officer Marlowe Dixon soon arrived. Dixon headed upstairs as Stan asked Liz, "Did you see anything unusual when you got back, before you noticed the door?"

Liz answered the chief's question. "Nothing seemed amiss when we returned from shopping. And Beans seemed okay with the world. But that's nothing new."

"You never know, though." Sadie dropped to her knees beside the snoring bulldog. "This could upset his digestion terribly."

Ignoring her, Liz asked the chief, "Is it all right if the others go home? Naomi and Caitlyn have early shifts tomorrow."

"And George will start to worry if I'm too late getting home," said Opal.

"Mary Ann or Sadie will have to check to see if anything's been stolen or damaged in Sew Welcome," the chief answered, "but I can call the rest of you tomorrow if necessary."

Liz hugged her departing friends, forcing a smile to her lips. "Thanks for a fun, special evening. Makes this so much more bearable."

"Let us know if you need anything," Naomi said, hugging her. She, Opal, and Caitlyn slipped out.

Liz, clasping Jackson's hand, led the chief to the door of her quarters.

The chief donned gloves and dusted for fingerprints. "Most of these are yours, I'm sure. Still, we might get lucky. You didn't go inside, did you?"

"Of course not."

"Didn't think so. If anyone would know better, it would be you. After I finish, we'll make sure nothing's missing."

His smartphone rang with an old-fashioned tone. He answered it, held a short conversation, then hung up. "Dixon says two guest rooms upstairs have been jimmied open."

She sighed. She'd have to check on that when they were done here and hope that none of her guests had been robbed.

Meanwhile, she focused on her quarters. When Stan gave her the go-ahead, Liz had to try her key several times because of the bent hardware. Finally, the lock clicked.

"Stand aside and wait out here." The chief flicked on a flashlight and put his hand on the gun in his belt as he entered. "Can't imagine the perp got in, but you can never be too careful."

Before long, he called, "All clear. Come on in, but try not to touch anything until I've finished."

He'd turned on several lights. As they entered, Liz and Jackson donned the gloves he gave them.

Stan said, "You have a safe inside here somewhere, don't you?"

She pointed. "Those wall panels slide apart. The safe's behind them."

Stan dusted them for fingerprints, then pushed the panels aside. "Doesn't look like anyone's tampered with it." He checked for fingerprints again. "Want to open it and make sure?"

She punched in its combination. The safe's door creaked open. A bag contained petty cash and other random monies, just as she had left them. Thank goodness she made a practice of locking all cash in the safe at day's end. No checks were missing, and no important papers were disturbed.

"It's all here."

"Good," the chief grunted as he scrutinized windowsills and closets.

Jackson gestured toward her laptop. "Glad you locked it up in here. If you'd left it at the front desk, the burglar might have taken it."

"I'm done, so you can see if anything else is missing." Stan whipped out his phone to make notes. "Maybe I'd better find out who all's been staying here."

"You met Geoffrey Teal from Nashville at coffee hour today." That enjoyable session seemed as if it had happened years ago. "Vanessa Leighton too. She's a business-supplies salesperson from Lansing." Liz added, "Both said they would be out this evening and return late."

"Anybody else?" The chief tapped away.

"Well, Terrence Pike, a professor, was here for two days to teach classes in Fort Wayne. But he checked out this morning and headed back to Cleveland."

She yanked open drawers and cabinets, but found nothing had been stolen. However, an Amish quilt had been taken from a rack in the rotunda, as well as a small antique vase.

"Valuable," Liz said, "but not irreplaceable." She was relieved that she usually kept her mother's quilt in her quarters.

Stan glanced toward the door separating the rotunda from the hallway to the kitchen and dining room. "I assume that door was locked too. And Sew Welcome's?"

"I *never* forget to lock our shop." Mary Ann raised her chin.

Sadie looked up from checking Beans's nose again. "Why would you even ask?"

"You know I have to." The chief called Dixon on his phone and then, after a short conversation, told Liz the officer hadn't found anything else unusual upstairs. "After we finish here, you'll have to go up and see if our perp's helped himself there. Your guests will need to do that too."

Liz sighed. Such a nice "welcome home" for Vanessa and Geoffrey.

As Officer Dixon descended from the guest rooms upstairs, Stan turned to Mary Ann and Sadie, gesturing toward Sew Welcome's door. "Dixon will check things out before you enter."

"Got it." They followed Dixon to their shop, the officer shaking his head as Sadie offered to fetch her shotgun from her car.

The twinkle in the chief's eye dissolved as he told Liz and Jackson, "I'm thinking the intruder got in through the utility room. I'll go in first and look things over, then let you know when you can come in. Keep your gloves on. Make minimal contact with surroundings, but keep your eyes open."

The minute Liz and Jackson entered the hallway, Liz knew the chief had confirmed his guess. An unfamiliar hallway draft grew into a brisk breeze as they entered the kitchen.

Shards of glass glittered on the floor by the utility room door. The chief shrugged. "The usual. Broke the door's window, then unlocked it and turned the deadbolt."

At first glance it appeared nothing had been taken, but closer examination revealed the thief had stolen small items from the dining room's buffet.

"He must have been in a hurry or traveling light." She pointed at her silver set. "Left the coffeepot, but took the sugar bowl and cream pitcher."

When no other thefts surfaced, they went upstairs. As Liz had feared, the burglar had broken into the Rose of Sharon Room, where Vanessa was staying.

But when they inspected the open Somewhere in Time Room where Liz had put Geoffrey, the chief's brows lowered again. "Surprised he didn't take some antique clocks."

Thankfully, the intruder seemed to have ignored the third floor.

Adrenaline had kept Liz moving throughout their search, but now, her rubbery legs barely carried her down the stairs.

"Can't Liz go to bed now?" Jackson asked the chief as he guided her to her desk chair.

"Fine with me. Dixon and I will wait for her guests to get back."

"Not fine with me." Dropping into the chair, Liz crossed her arms. "Let Vanessa and Geoffrey walk in to find only the police? I don't think so."

Jackson frowned. "At least lie down in the sitting room. I'll tell you when they come."

"Okay. After Mary Ann and Sadie tell us if their shop's all right." She summoned the best smile she could manage.

Five minutes later, the partners reappeared. "No break-in, no theft," Mary Ann reported.

As Mary Ann and Sadie were exiting the front door, however, Vanessa entered and spotted the officers. "What on earth?"

Liz introduced them. When she suggested they go into the library, Jackson offered to temporarily secure the utility room door using supplies from the garage while she and the chief explained the situation. He left to do so.

Vanessa's eyes widened as she stared from Liz to Stan. "I might expect this in Lansing, but not here!"

The chief cleared his throat. "Unfortunately, crimes also happen in small towns, Ms. Leighton."

He accompanied her upstairs so she could check her belongings.

When they returned, she'd lost a gold necklace with a diamond pendant and matching earrings from her jewelry box. "Fortunately, I took my bag and notebook computer to my meeting."

"Vanessa, I'm so sorry," Liz said sincerely.

Her guest managed a smile. "I am too. But don't worry, Liz. I bought those pieces on clearance and I have a jewelry rider on my insurance. There's no sentimental value."

The chief asked Vanessa specifics about her meeting. She gave him the customer's name and contact information, plus the Fort Wayne restaurant where they'd met.

After Stan dismissed her, Vanessa asked Liz, "Do you have another room available tonight?" Lines had gathered around her mouth, and she looked weary.

"Certainly." Liz scurried to fetch keys to the Amish Room. "You're welcome to use it for the remainder of your stay."

Please don't leave. Though she wouldn't have blamed her, Liz couldn't afford to lose guests.

Thankfully, Vanessa didn't mention a departure.

"I promise we'll have a patrol car checking the premises several times tonight," the chief told her.

Vanessa's acceptance of the situation made telling Geoffrey, when he arrived, much easier. His main concern was whether Liz had been at home during the robbery.

"Thank goodness," was his response when he was reassured that she had been out.

After checking his room with Officer Dixon, Geoffrey readily supplied the chief with the name of the friend with whom he'd spent the evening and his phone number. "I can't believe we were jamming while all this was going on."

When he finally retired, Jackson turned to Liz. "*Now* will you go to bed?"

She nodded. "You go home too. I'll be fine."

He gave her a concerned look, but kissed her good night and left.

Falling asleep sounded like mission impossible. She lay awake for what seemed forever, but finally drifted into a shallow, jumpy slumber.

Geoffrey shouldn't have. He *really* shouldn't have bought her this expensive-looking gold box of truffles.

Vanessa had left for the day. Geoffrey had helped Liz and Sarah, Liz's part-time Amish assistant, clear breakfast dishes, then with a flourish, he'd returned to the dining room to present the box to Liz, who was doing some additional cleanup.

"I had no idea you'd be recovering from a burglary." He flashed his too-bright smile. "But perhaps chocolate will make it a little better?"

"I appreciate your thoughtfulness," Liz continued, "but these gifts truly aren't necessary. You're a paying guest."

He looked crestfallen. Would he pack up and leave? Liz's spreadsheets flashed through her mind—as well as an online review about the Olde Mansion Inn's touchy owner.

Instead, when Geoffrey raised his eyes, they held an odd smile. "I'm so sorry, Liz. I seem to have made you uncomfortable, which was not my intention. I was just so pleased to finally meet you."

Somehow she didn't think her reputation for hospitality reached *that* far. "Well, I'm pleased to meet you too." What else could she say?

His smile widened. "You have no idea how happy that makes me." He leaned forward and reached out, almost as if he were about to take one of Liz's hands. But, apparently noticing Liz's surprise, he drew back almost immediately.

"I almost overstepped there, and again, I'm sorry. But now that we're alone, I may as well spit out the real reason I'm here."

Liz's antennae went up. Sarah was in the kitchen, thank goodness, so they weren't truly alone. She cleared her throat and summoned up her Lawyer Liz persona. "Perhaps you'd better tell me what you mean, Geoffrey."

"It's not what you think. I don't, uh, want to date you or anything. Jackson seems like a stand-up guy, and I'm happy for you two."

Well that was a relief. But what possible other reason could there be for Geoffrey's attentions? "Then what is it?"

"It's family, Liz." His stare probed hers. "I'm your father's brother. Your uncle."

4

"Brother?" The word fell from Liz's lips awkwardly, as if she were saying it for the first time and wasn't sure about the pronunciation. "Uncle?"

Geoffrey nodded. "I should have waited awhile before telling you, but I was so excited to have found you."

She remembered that family-less feeling way too well. But the familiar twinge didn't right the room, which seemed to be tilted sideways. "I-I think I'll sit down."

He pushed a chair toward her. "I don't blame you. I was floored too, though"—his voice faded to wistfulness—"I was a little happier about it."

"B-but how can you be my uncle?" The word still clogged Liz's brain and mouth. "You're my age, aren't you? Around forty?" Actually, he possessed fewer wrinkles.

"A few years older. And it's not impossible, just complicated."

Of course it was possible. Though right now, anything seemed possible. "I need more coffee."

"I'll get it for you. Vanilla-flavored, right? A little cream?"

"Um, yeah."

Geoffrey loped off to the sitting room coffee machine.

Maybe he needed breathing space too. Liz inhaled several times. But her hands still gripped the chair as if she were flying in a space shuttle.

Her father had died too young for Liz to have known him well. Her mother had given her his photo. The fun-loving man had teased her serious mother into laughter. He'd filled their lives with music, playing guitar and keyboards, she recalled in a shadowy memory.

But Mark Eckardt had remained a storybook figure throughout her lifetime, bigger than life, yet unreal.

As Liz's wedding neared, she'd missed her father.

Now this stranger had appeared. A stranger with dark hair like Dad's. Blue eyes like his.

Like hers.

If only Mom were here. Liz ached for her mother's touch, her guidance.

But Mom had said Liz's father had no living relatives.

Abigail Eckardt had always told the truth. Always.

Geoffrey, carrying two steaming coffees, interrupted her spinning thoughts.

Liz inhaled her mug's comforting aroma while he sat across from her. She couldn't escape Geoffrey's hopeful glance.

He said, "Do you have time to hear the whole story? It's rather . . . involved."

"I can make time." She wouldn't accomplish anything this morning, anyway, after this bombshell. "Shoot."

The light slowly drained from his face. "The whole thing started when my dad died."

"I'm sorry." Questions leaped to her lips, but Liz quieted them. For now.

"Thanks." He bit his lip. "I was trying to help my mother, so I cleared out the attic. Mom must have forgotten about old letters from a childhood friend. Letters that asked about her first husband and the baby boy she'd had at nineteen."

Liz's breath caught in her throat.

"A baby they'd named Mark." His breath quickened. "The whole time I was growing up, I'd hated being an only child. But now, I had a brother!"

Geoffrey's joy both lifted and frightened her. "What was your mother's reaction? What's her name? Is she still living?"

She was using her lawyer voice, she realized.

His elation dried up. "Well, counselor, I suppose I expected questions. First, my mother's name is Anita Teal—Anita Fuller Teal." He held out some documents for her.

One was her father's baptismal certificate.

Liz read slowly, carefully. It recorded the baptism of Mark Edward Fuller, born on July 9, more than sixty years before, to Anita Anne Fuller and Eddie James Fuller. He'd been baptized at Trinity Methodist Church, Bass Hollow, Tennessee.

The other was an original birth certificate that documented Geoffrey Daniel Teal's birth to Anita Fuller Teal and Jon Michael Teal in Lexington, Kentucky.

"Mom said they got married right after high school, and soon after Mark was born a year later, her husband was killed in a work accident. When she couldn't afford to care for Mark properly, and with no family to turn to, she made the heart-wrenching decision to give him up for adoption." Geoffrey shook his head. "Losing both of them must have really hurt her. Mom waited years before she married Dad and had me."

Liz took the plunge. "Did she tell your dad about mine?"

Geoffrey looked away. "No. He knew she'd been married before, but never knew about Mark. You asked about her reaction to my finding those letters. It wasn't good."

Not surprising. A grieving widow probably wouldn't welcome explaining such a painful past to her son.

A grieving widow who might be Liz's grandmother.

Liz caught her breath. "Where is your mother?"

His face stiffened. "I don't know."

"She's so angry she won't speak to you?" Liz couldn't imagine disowning a son for seeking his brother.

"No, not angry." Geoffrey's chin sank. "After Dad died, Mom suffered depression that grew worse every day. Nothing helped. She got upset when I discovered her letters, but she still talked to me. Actually, Mom seemed more like herself when we argued about my looking for Mark." A tiny smile, like a moth, flitted across his face, then died. "I stayed with her for weeks, trying to help her. One morning, I woke up, and she was gone."

"Gone?" The word slipped out before Liz could stop it.

Geoffrey gritted his teeth. "I found a brochure for a Mediterranean cruise and I think that's where she might be, but the cruise line isn't confirming one way or another whether she's on their boat. I've checked with friends, homeless shelters, hospitals—you name it—all over the country. She did send two e-mails that she was okay, calling me by a pet name only she would know." He looked away. "I just want to know she's okay."

Seized with longing to know her grandmother, Liz fought the urge to hug him. Was he telling the truth?

Finally, he spoke. "I won't stop trying to find her. But if she doesn't want to be found . . ." His eyes moistened, but the corners of his mouth slowly curved upward. "Well, that makes me especially glad I found you."

Can this really be true?

"It's not enough that we had a break-in. Now I have to deal with this. I didn't know what to say to Geoffrey. I didn't know what to do." Jackson had appeared soon after Geoffrey left Liz and now they walked hand in hand along the lake, Liz endeavoring to absorb the September morning's golden peace. "I hated to leave him hanging."

"You did exactly the right thing. You listened. You didn't overreact or jump to conclusions."

"I know what it's like to lose a parent, like Geoffrey lost his dad. I know what it's like to feel alone, without a family." The forest trail's tranquil greenness seemed to mock her mood.

"You're not alone now. Whatever happens, I'll help you through this." Jackson squeezed her hand.

"I know you will." She picked up the pace. "I just wish Geoffrey hadn't shown up right before our wedding."

"Bearing chocolates, no less." Jackson's teasing told Liz he'd taken no offense at her maybe-uncle's gift. "Guess I'd better shape up if I want to compete with this guy."

"He couldn't begin to compete with you." She tried to match his attempt at lightness. "But I'm glad I decided to keep the truffles, after all."

"Eat 'em up," Jackson urged. "They'll help you through the day."

"But in only a few weeks, I'll have to fit into my dress. Maybe I'll only eat half the box." Liz attempted a chuckle. "It'll be a busy day. More guests are arriving this afternoon."

"You'll start checking out Geoffrey's claim too." A statement, not a question.

"First, I'd better get my father's background straight." Liz sighed. "Mom told me that Dad had been adopted by the Eckardt family. She said he sometimes struggled with being adopted. But when I went through her files after she died, I never saw any documentation of Dad's birth or adoption."

Liz frowned. "From what I've gathered about their relationship, I believe my father would have told Mom if he had a sibling. And I'm sure she would have told me. But if he didn't know, he couldn't have told her." She steadied her voice. "Adoption was very different back then. All ties with a person's birth family were cut. Records were closed. Perhaps my father had tried to trace his mother, but couldn't—especially if she didn't want to be found." Geoffrey's similar words floated through her mind. Had her father shared sadness akin to his brother's?

Jackson squeezed her hand. "I know you'll find it hard to lay this aside for even a moment."

"Especially with Geoffrey around." Thank goodness he had a gig tonight.

"But will you try not to obsess about it?"

"Me? Obsess?" She laid a hand on her chest in mock outrage. "How could you imagine such a thing?"

He snorted. "Because I know you. You're more of a bulldog than Beans will ever be."

"Whoa, how romantic is that? Tell me more sweet nothings."

"You know what I mean. As you said, you already have to deal with the break-in. You don't need to obsess about Geoffrey."

Liz didn't want to agree, so she countered, "I might go to Miriam's this afternoon." After she'd called the county offices that covered records for Bass Hollow, Tennessee.

He looked relieved. "Good idea. Get away for a while." They returned to the inn in companionable silence, and Jackson left her at the front door.

Watching him stride toward downtown, Liz pulled out her phone. Pulse quickening, she began to search the Internet for Tennessee's child services website.

5

The ensuing phone calls were supposed to open the door to her father's background.

Instead, Liz hit a brick wall.

As requested, she faxed a copy of her own birth certificate to prove their kinship. Her child services contact quickly called back—with bad news.

"Your father was born before 1960?" More than a tinge of regret colored the Southern woman's voice. "Our offices were housed in the courthouse then. It burned in 1962. Or was it '63? Most of the county clerk's records and our adoption records burned with it. No backup or off-site storage then. Gracious, they didn't even bother with mimeographs." She clicked her tongue. "I'm afraid I can't help you, hon. I'm so sorry."

A call to the county clerk's office confirmed the child services woman's information. "Yes, that fire has caused a heap of problems. I can't find a Mark Edward Fuller with that birth date in our records. But that doesn't mean he wasn't born here. He may have been born at home, and nobody told us, which often happened back then. I imagine your daddy, after he grew up, worked this out with a lawyer, using adoption information, to obtain a birth certificate."

Liz's temples tightened as she hung up. Anita Fuller might have given birth to Liz's father on a farm near Bass Hollow, a town hardly bigger than its dot on the map.

Still, someone at nearby hospitals might know something about orphanages or benevolence societies that handled adoptions during the 1950s.

Liz spent the rest of the morning on the phone, with no positive results. No one in either hospital in the county could answer her questions. Liz had hoped to encounter at least a promising thread of evidence to support Geoffrey's claim. What would she say to him? Coffee hour would be awkward today.

Her nagging stomach reminded her she'd forgotten to eat lunch. Grabbing a sandwich and an apple, Liz ate absentmindedly as she drove to Miriam's farm.

She *needed* Miriam today. Liz's cousin and her family were proof positive Liz had previously tracked down family members. When she pulled into their gravel driveway, Miriam would appear on the big house's porch, her face under her black *Kapp* aglow with a welcoming smile.

That knowledge—plus her blood sugar inching upward—helped soothe Liz's mild headache. By the time she arrived at Miriam's, the day looked brighter.

After she and Miriam had rocked on the porch in the sunshine with big slices of shoofly pie, everything seemed entirely manageable. Her cousin's colorful garden, ablaze with nasturtiums and a fall planting of peas, lifted Liz's spirits. How could she remain gloomy when Miriam's daughters, Grace and little Keturah, shared their smiles as well?

After the girls headed to the haymow to play, Liz told Miriam about the break-in.

"Oh, Liz, please be careful."

"I am. The police are patrolling around the inn at night. And guests are staying with me."

Liz also told her about Geoffrey's revelation.

Miriam's indigo eyes widened. "But didn't your mother say that your father had no living relatives?"

"She did. I can only assume she didn't know about Geoffrey." Liz bit her lip. "I hope I can find the documentation I need. I'd like to believe we're related. I'd love to have an uncle at my wedding. But I can't swallow every claim from every person who shows up at my inn."

"Of course not." Miriam's calm gaze searched Liz's face. "Do you think he expects you to?"

Liz shrugged. "I don't know. Probably not, though he seems excited about our being related."

"Perhaps you are the one who is pressuring you." A tiny smile tugged at Miriam's mouth.

Without insinuating Liz was a bulldog, she had echoed Jackson's insights.

What was it about Miriam that eased the tightness of the iron band of worry around Liz's head? It was a connection that, despite their differences, had existed from the moment they met.

The power of family.

No wonder lonely, grieving Geoffrey had tried so hard to find her. No wonder she herself longed for a bond with her father's family that she now enjoyed with her mother's.

The serenity Liz had absorbed from Miriam—so similar to Liz's mother's—gave her the composure to face Geoffrey's situation in a realistic way. Their kinship might prove genuine, but if it didn't, Liz still considered herself fortunate.

An hour later, Liz returned to the inn, ready to welcome more guests with her spirit soothed and her head on straight.

Brandon and Danielle Henson, a trendy young couple from Chicago, had come to escape urban pressures.

"I hope you'll enjoy the Heritage Room." Liz attempted to hand them its keys.

Neither raised their eyes from their phones.

Liz tapped the counter with the keys. Danielle finally took them.

Watching both visitors navigate the rotunda stairs, gazes glued to devices, Liz wondered if after the weekend, they would recall where they'd been.

Phyllis and Pinky Pembroke, a mother-daughter duo, more than made up for the Hensons' silence. Tiny and dark-eyed, they chittered like sparrows.

"Coffee hour? How lovely—"

"Only two cups, Mama, you know—"

"I don't care if he is a smart man, that doctor doesn't—"

"But Dr. Spratt is so nice—"

"This is my vacation—"

"We can't wait to see the Amish—"

"I've always wanted to take a buggy ride!"

You finished a sentence? Liz thought.

Apparently, one was enough. After she gave them keys to the Sunrise and Sunset rooms on the third floor, the two scurried up the stairs with their small, neat luggage, still talking.

The silence left in their wake filled the rotunda. How had Pinky acquired her nickname? According to the register, her given name was Evangeline. Would the verbal tag team ever allow Liz to get in a word edgewise and ask?

Slowly collecting her thoughts, Liz baked pumpkin bars for coffee hour, slathering them with cream cheese frosting.

Sadie and Mary Ann, with their standing invitation, regarded Friday's coffee time as their happy hour, often trading off.

Today, Mary Ann arrived before any of Liz's guests. Thank goodness. While Sadie often kept visitors laughing with outrageous remarks, her boisterous personality occasionally rubbed guests the wrong way. Mary Ann was a much safer choice, with her polite questions that made people feel comfortable telling her their life stories.

"So, Liz." Her friend popped a blackberry tea pod into the

machine and pressed the button to start the brew. "What can I do to help with Geoffrey?"

"Jackson told you." She hadn't exactly sworn him to secrecy. In a way, she was glad he'd confided in Mary Ann. Jackson's mother, Therese, had come to appreciate Liz. However, this new twist in her future daughter-in-law's background might cause kinks in their still-fragile relationship.

"Naturally." Mary Ann helped herself to a pumpkin bar. "He's concerned about you. So are we."

"We," meaning her and Sadie. And the rest of the Material Girls. Liz sighed. The Pleasant Creek grapevine would spread the news to most of the town.

Thankfully, out-of-town guests didn't know about this development. The Hensons, both wearing earbuds and step counters, thanked Liz for the pumpkin bars, hurried outside, and marched toward the lake path.

The Pembrokes chatted with Vanessa, who handled their alternating onslaughts with grace.

When Geoffrey arrived, he tried to make conversation with the ladies, but the Pembrokes deluged him with the plots of their favorite novels. Though polite, he made it abundantly clear that he hated to read.

Enter Jackson, who rescued Geoffrey. Mary Ann did the same for Vanessa, who appeared to have had enough of the book conversation. She and Liz enjoyed discussing area restaurants. Vanessa recommended Earth's Bountiful Table, one that emphasized using local produce.

Jackson must have overheard their chat. "Liz, I forgot to tell you that the county council gave us a gift certificate for that place."

She'd love to leave all the family controversy and wedding details behind and spend an evening there with him. "Maybe we can set aside an evening to go later this fall."

Though she'd exchanged quick hugs and polite conversation with Geoffrey, Liz hadn't had to deal with heavy subjects. For that she was grateful. He, too, seemed satisfied with simply sharing a few meaningful glances with her. *No pressure*, his expression read. *I'm just glad to be here.*

She relayed her own openness—she hoped—and permitted herself to view the weekend optimistically. From what Geoffrey had said earlier, various gigs would keep him busy through Labor Day. If the Hensons continued in their cyber world, they'd require little attention. Vanessa, her business concluded, was checking out tomorrow morning. If the Pembroke women visited half the local points of interest they'd listed in their verbal itineraries, they wouldn't expect Liz to keep them company.

Perhaps she might accomplish more wedding tasks than she'd anticipated. She and Jackson might even get to relax instead of running errands. As if sensing her gaze from across the room, her husband-to-be turned and smiled.

Only a few more weeks. Then, even when life took insane turns, they could navigate the craziness together.

In that lovely, euphoric moment, Steve walked in.

His presence lifted her heart. After years of dangerous military service, she rejoiced that Steve was home, safe and sound. Today, though, he half-raised his open hand in a sort-of greeting, then turned an eye on Geoffrey.

Had Steve heard about the musician's claim to be Liz's uncle? She should have told him. But Geoffrey had approached her only this morning. Surely the town grapevine didn't work *that* quickly.

Mary Ann scooted to Steve's side. With the buzz of conversation, Liz couldn't hear what she said, but she coaxed a smile from him.

Should I or shouldn't I? Liz wanted to join them, but her direct participation might cause tension. She'd talk with Steve later. She hoped.

In refilling cookie plates and drink supplies, Liz occasionally touched Steve's elbow or patted his shoulder as she passed. He gave her a half-smile. Whatever her supposed sin, Steve didn't consider it unforgiveable. Her plan to talk with him after coffee hour dissolved, though, when he stood and walked out the sitting room door.

Liz dashed after Steve and planted herself firmly in front of him. "Did I say something, hon? Do something?"

He gave a dry chuckle. "No, Mom, you didn't do anything wrong."

"Then why the . . . whatever-this-is?" She gestured vaguely at him.

He paused. "The problem is, I think you're too trusting." Steve shifted his gaze back through the sitting room door. "I wish Geoffrey wasn't staying in your inn. He's up to something."

Liz blinked. "You don't even know him. Why would you think such a thing?"

"It's just a feeling. A strong one."

Her son strode out the inn's entrance, leaving Liz to stare after him and wonder. Perplexed, Liz began collecting mugs and teacups. Jackson helped her.

"Wish I didn't have this conference to go to. At least it's only overnight." He raised an eyebrow at her. "Do you think you can stay out of trouble while I'm gone?"

"I hope so." She'd forgotten about his mayors' conference. "Maybe we can meet for dinner tomorrow night when you get back."

Mary Ann had edged the garrulous Pembrokes toward the sitting room door. Now she expertly eased them into the rotunda, then toward the stairway. Vanessa had already left to meet a friend in Marion for dinner. Only Geoffrey remained to help them gather trash, napkins, and spoons.

Her guest grinned at Jackson. "You're soon going to be doing double duty, aren't you? Both mayor stuff and inn stuff?"

"Triple, actually," Liz chimed in. "Jackson owns a furniture factory and store too." She smiled at her fiancé. "But he can handle it."

"I'll do my best, and of course, I'll help out around here. But the inn is Liz's business—and she runs it extremely well." Jackson hugged Liz, then waved to Geoffrey and headed out the door.

Geoffrey said, "He's a good man. I'm so glad for you, Liz."

"I'm glad for me too." His comment had warmed her, but Liz wanted to keep some distance between them.

As if sensing her desire to steer away from personal subjects, Geoffrey said, "The pumpkin bars were great." He tilted his head like a wistful ten-year-old. "But do you think we might have poppy seed bread for tomorrow's coffee hour? It's incredible."

"Sure." Appreciation was always nice. "In fact, I might have spare loaves in the freezer. Remind me to give you one."

"Thanks!"

He left soon afterward, with no reference to the elephant-size question between them.

Her sigh of relief as she headed for the kitchen degenerated into one of worry. Had Geoffrey sensed Steve's disapproval? Was Steve right about him?

Loading the dishwasher drained her last ounce of energy. Hot cider sounded good. She heated a cup of Amish-made cider and carried it to the four-season room.

Liz sat on the rattan sofa and rested her feet on an ottoman, gazing at the lake. Usually, its rippled sky murals eased her tensions and blood pressure. This evening, though, its beauty only emphasized that she couldn't share it with anyone.

Liz toyed with her phone. But everyone had mentioned plans for tonight.

With Jackson gone as well as her guests, quiet seeped into every corner of the four- season room. Though she tried to push away the thought, Liz wondered where Steve was . . . and why he judged Geoffrey so harshly.

Even reading a favorite novel wouldn't scare away that ghost. Liz jumped to her feet, hurried to open the door to her quarters, and grabbed her mother's diary from her purse. And the truffles Geoffrey had given her.

If she couldn't eat chocolate with her mother, at least Liz could savor her words again.

She returned to the four-season room, unwrapped a mocha latte truffle, and opened the diary. For a moment, Abigail Eckardt's neat handwriting blurred. Liz dabbed away a tear, but as she reread the diary, her mother's brave, eighteen-year-old naïveté brought smiles too. Liz relived her mother's astonishment as she worked at one of the only jobs her Amish eighth-grade education permitted—Santa's elf at a Boston mall.

I have exchanged my Kapp for a sparkly green elf hat, Abigail wrote. *Sometimes I wonder if I not only have settled in a new state, but on a different planet.*

Poor Mom. Arriving in Boston at Christmas must have proved an enormous adjustment—as had her enrollment in GED courses, then at a junior college. Abigail had met Liz's father there.

She smiled at her mother's insistence that they were only friends. When Mark began to share his music with her, though, Deborah's efforts to distance herself waned. At the bottom of one page, Liz read:

I've stopped running from love, you're the rose that lasts,

I've stopped running from love, stronger than my past.

Liz inhaled.

The words nearly matched the lyrics of Trey Edmond's song.

Except they lauded a strong love that would last. It was the perfect verse for the wedding.

Her mother had recorded those lines in her diary more than forty years before. That song wasn't brand new, no matter what the DJs said.

Liz dropped back against the sofa, listening as someone hummed a melody with intermittent words in her mind. The faraway, off-key tune made Liz wince, yet wrapped her in love.

Stopped running . . . hmmm . . . rose that lasts

Stopped shunning . . . hmmm . . . stronger than my past.

The past. A wisp of a memory floated through her mind. Her mother's voice, singing to Liz when she was very small.

Her mother singing this very song.

6

It seemed Liz had barely fallen asleep when her alarm shouted its unreasonable demand.

She crawled out of bed and grabbed her mother's diary from her nightstand. Though she'd spent half the night rereading it, Liz wanted to see them again—the lyrics to her wedding song inside the back of the diary. The verse Trey Edmond hadn't sung.

I've stopped running from love, you're the rose that lasts,

I've stopped running from love, stronger than my past.

You are the love Love sent to me

To help set me free

To take me home

And make me her own forever.

Love, you are my friend.

Love, you are my friend.

How had she missed this with all the times she'd read the diary? She must have brushed over it, thinking her intelligent but unimaginative mother had copied a poem she admired, which she sometimes did. Now she wondered: Had this been her parents' wedding song?

She looked at their pictures on her dresser—her mother, smiling and happy, standing arm in arm with Dad, a young man who would never get much older than he was in the photo.

They *must* have chosen this song. And Liz now wanted the entire song to be sung at their wedding. She'd talk to Jackson about it tonight.

A faint chime of the rotunda grandfather clock made her check the time. Were the Pembrokes early birds? Or the Hensons? She'd better start breakfast soon. Her hands still trembled as she threw on her clothes. Sarah had the morning off so she was on her own.

Knock it off, Liz. It's only a song.

But finding it in her mom's diary made her feel as if her parents were speaking to her, urging her to choose it. As her wedding approached, she'd missed them both so much . . .

A note stuck to the kitchen door brought her back to earth. Geoffrey wrote that he wasn't eating breakfast at the inn. *But I'd like us to get to know each other a little better. Coffee with me around two? My treat.*

The note sent the song lyrics to her mind's back burner as she fried bacon and mixed pancake batter. She couldn't pursue more evidence to support or disprove Geoffrey's claim, not until after Labor Day weekend. He'd probably attempt to charm her into accepting him. Yet, if Geoffrey was indeed her uncle, she didn't want to push him away. Nor did she want to sabotage a vital link to her maybe-grandmother, Anita.

My grandmother.

Though she'd sung with other grade-schoolers about going "over the river and through the woods," Liz had never gone to Grandmother's house. Her mother had come to every school function she'd had growing up, but she'd never looked into an audience and been reassured by twinkling eyes in a weathered face.

A distinct burning smell interrupted her reverie.

"Ack!" Liz grabbed a spatula and flipped too-crispy pancakes.

Mary Ann and Sadie, who also frequented the inn's Saturday morning breakfasts, bustled into the kitchen.

Sadie eyed Liz's pancakes. "Are you going to feed those to somebody?"

"Me." Liz tapped one's dark top. "Maybe."

Sadie flipped the pancakes neatly into the trash. "You wouldn't serve those to me. I won't let you serve them to yourself."

"She's right, dear." Mary Ann hugged Liz as Sadie poured more batter onto the griddle. "You've got too much on your mind. Sadie will do pancakes, I'll round up your toppings and bacon, and you can take care of everything else."

Outwardly obedient, Liz headed for the dining room to fill the cream pitcher, arrange china, and fold more napkins.

She gave thanks for her friends' mom-like presence.

Mom. Liz stopped mid fold. How had she forgotten to mention the lyrics in her mother's diary?

She turned toward the kitchen, but the Pembrokes fluttered into the dining room. The Hensons, toting backpacks, looked ready to eat and run, so Liz greeted everyone and poured first cups of coffee, then scurried back to the kitchen.

Mmm. Mouthwatering piles of bacon and stacks of fluffy golden pancakes awaited her, with a large pitcher of hot maple syrup and bowls of warm apple topping, chocolate chips, sliced bananas, and whipped cream. "You two are the best."

"We know," Sadie said lightly, earning herself an elbow in the ribs from Mary Ann.

Mary Ann and Sadie helped Liz carry the breakfast to her guests, seated around the big mahogany table. Even Phyllis and Pinky quieted as they dug in. Fortunately, Vanessa appeared before all the pancakes vanished.

With each bite, Liz's guests seemed to relax. The Hensons hung around, even speaking occasionally, though they texted nonstop—mostly to each other, judging by their sidelong glances.

People, you're sitting together!

The Pembroke women paused to sip coffee and occasionally listen to the rest. Knowing Mary Ann and Sadie soon would leave to open Sew Welcome, Liz told them about the "Love, You Are My Friend" lyrics in the diary.

Mary Ann flashed her brilliant smile. "I knew there was something special about that song. It's perfect for your wedding!"

"The song you played when we were quilting?" Vanessa asked. "Beautiful."

"Yes, it is," Liz agreed with a smile. "But even better, I was right when I thought it ended with lasting love. That's the way my mother sang it to me when I was little." Liz grinned. "Or tried to sing. Mom was tone-deaf."

Phyllis and Pinky interrupted with ecstatic congratulations and tag-team questions about Liz's groom, wedding colors, and reception plans. The Hensons avoided the barrage by leaving. Vanessa, who needed to pack, eventually exchanged goodbyes and left too.

Thankful that Vanessa's checkout gave her an excuse to end the conversation, Liz helped the saleswoman carry her bags downstairs after checking her out.

"Please come back and see us," Liz urged.

"I'll be in the area again soon, so I may do that." Vanessa hugged her.

Later, as Liz scrubbed bathrooms and folded towels, though, Geoffrey's note niggled at her. He'd asked to have coffee at two. Would she go?

Instead, maybe she'd unearth "essential business" that had to be resolved that afternoon. In Marion. Or Fort Wayne.

Or Timbuktu.

Yeah, running away will solve everything.

Even if she avoided Geoffrey all weekend and sent him off with nothing more than poppy seed bread, questions would pelt her with all the mercilessness of the Pembrokes' conversations. Liz closed the now-clean Amish Room's door with a thump.

She'd meet Geoffrey for coffee. Maybe one of Naomi's luscious key lime cupcakes would sweeten the ordeal.

Geoffrey showed up promptly at two and agreed to go to Sweet Everything. "I imagine you need to get away sometimes."

"Occasionally, I like someone else to pour my coffee."

Exchanging chitchat about Pleasant Creek's buggy traffic and the hitching rails alongside parking meters, they walked to Sweet Everything.

The bakery's soothing gray walls and cheerful coral place mats and accents always lifted Liz's spirits. Today autumnal sunflower-and-wheatgrass arrangements brightened every table and booth.

After taking their order, Naomi raised her brows slightly, silently notifying Liz that Mary Ann and Sadie had filled her in about Geoffrey. Liz gave a slight nod, acknowledging the concern she knew Naomi felt. Later, she'd fill her friend in on details and catch up on Naomi's date the previous night.

It was so good to have good friends. She'd enjoyed her Boston buds, but none had shared life with her like those here. However, hometown stares targeted her and Geoffrey as they walked to an empty booth. Did they already know about Geoffrey's claim to be her uncle? She stirred cream into her coffee. She should have known better than to bring Geoffrey here.

He murmured, "Guess I'm a real object of interest."

"Sorry. One of the inconveniences of living in a small town."

"It's heartwarming, in a way." He smiled. "I can tell these people care about you. If I made one wrong move, they'd come after me."

Naomi, bringing their coffee and cupcakes, said, "You'd better believe it."

Liz laughed. "It's an inconvenience I've learned to appreciate."

"We take care of our own." Naomi leveled a smiling but unyielding gaze at Geoffrey, while asking if they wanted anything else. Since there was nothing more, she moved on to the next table.

Liz fiddled with her cup, then blurted, "How did you find my father?"

"You get right to the point, don't you?"

"Especially when it involves family." Liz pulled out her phone and prepared to take notes. Geoffrey willingly reviewed the names and dates he'd already given her.

Liz continued, "After you discovered those letters in your mother's attic, how did you find him? Did your mother give you details?"

"A few. After she quit yelling at me and crying." He grimaced, then continued, "The first few years after Mark's birth, Mom kept tabs on him through a caseworker who didn't like the laws that closed the books for birth parents. Mom found out he'd been adopted by a family named Eckardt, a minister and his wife who lived in a different town."

Though neither Liz nor her mother had ever met her father's adoptive parents—they'd both died when he was in his late teens—her mother had told Liz that her paternal grandfather had been a pastor. So far, still consistent.

"Mom scraped together enough money to take the bus there twice," Geoffrey paused. "She attended the minister's church so she could catch a glimpse of the son she'd felt she had no choice but to give up."

The picture of a teen mom stealing glances at her child twisted Liz's insides. "Go on."

"After several years, the worker told Mom the minister had been transferred to Boston." Geoffrey shook his head. "To a country girl from Tennessee, New England sounded as far away as Mars. She figured she'd never see Mark again. And she hasn't." He exhaled. "Glad she knew something about him, though, especially his adopted last name. When I was trying to track Mark, I found out a fire during the 1960s had destroyed a bunch of records, including his."

The same courthouse fire she'd discovered during her phone calls. Liz's pulse quickened. "Where did you get the baptismal certificate?"

"I was kind of lucky." His face brightened. "Talked on the phone to a nice little old lady who sent it to me right before the church closed."

Closed? "Do you remember her name? Can you give me her number?"

"Lettie Starks. But the next time I tried to call her with questions, the line was disconnected. I found her obituary online."

Another brick wall. Both she and Geoffrey seemed to encounter more than their share of those when trying to find family. "How did you find my father in Boston?"

"It was harder than I expected." Geoffrey stirred more sugar into his coffee. "Since Mark's father was a minister, I figured his denominational offices could tell me where he pastored. They did, but both he and his wife had died years before. I hoped obituaries would tell me where Mark was living. But he'd been a college student at the time, and the post-graduation addresses the school gave led me nowhere."

Liz couldn't remember her mother ever receiving mail from her alma mater. "How did you finally find my dad?"

"I joined websites where people were looking for relatives. Eventually, a guy named Theo Bronson posted that he'd attended the same church as Mark a long time ago." Geoffrey's eyes moistened. "But when he told me Mark had died in an accident, I was heartbroken."

Liz stared down at her untouched cupcake. "How did you find out about me?"

"You were a baby when they were friends. Theo, who moved a year after Mark died, said he'd heard your mother continued at that church for years."

Yes, they'd attended the same church ever since Liz could remember.

Geoffrey continued, "I went to see the pastor and showed him Mark's baptismal certificate and my birth certificate, and he told me you'd moved to Pleasant Creek, Indiana. So I lined up gigs in this area, and here I am." A small smile hovered on his lips. "Whether you're glad or not, I'm glad I found you."

"Why?" Liz tried to keep her voice from breaking. "Why did you go to all this trouble?"

"You, of all people, are asking that?" Geoffrey stared at her. "Didn't you leave everything in Boston to find your mother's family?"

"Well, yes—"

"My dad just died. Who knows where my mom is? I don't have kids. All I have are a couple of nasty ex-wives and my father's siblings, who don't seem all that interested in knowing me." Geoffrey bit his lip. "I want family, Liz. Is that so hard to understand?"

"No. No it isn't." She took a deep breath. "But I'm a lawyer, Geoffrey, and I need to double-check these facts. I also need time to digest all this."

"I get that," he said quietly. He glanced over her shoulder and frowned. "I also get that your son will need lots of time to process this."

"He has been . . . struggling with it." The watchfulness in Geoffrey's face triggered her inner alarm. "Did Steve come in?"

"I don't know when he entered, but he's sitting on the other side of the room."

Maybe Steve had dropped in for coffee. But he was trying to avoid sweets, and he preferred the coffee at Mama's Home Cooking. Had Steve followed them to Sweet Everything?

Geoffrey winced. "He sure doesn't look happy."

Liz closed her eyes. She and Steve needed to talk. "Maybe we'd better put this whole thing on hold for a while."

Geoffrey nodded. "I don't want to cause any trouble." He glanced at his watch. "I'll skip coffee hour and go early to my gig."

"I'll walk you to the door, then sit with Steve."

Her son, however, already had stood when she approached his table.

"I see you're leaving." Liz summoned her best smile. "Maybe I could walk with you?"

Steve hesitated. "Mom, I know you want to talk. But I should hurry back to Jackson's store. He needs my help. He's . . . been gone a lot lately."

Jackson certainly had lost time at work—helping her. Liz ventured, "How about getting together tomorrow evening? Maybe about five?" Geoffrey would be off to another performance by then.

"Okay, I guess."

He gave her a quick hug, then ducked out the door. She was thankful to see Steve walking downtown toward Jackson's furniture store and not toward Geoffrey as he returned to the inn.

Liz quickly exited and watched from the sidewalk until she could be sure neither planned to circle the block and confront the other. Naomi's warm hand on her shoulder felt like the best thing that had happened that day. As Liz turned, her friend held up a small white bag. "Want your cupcake to go?"

For once, Liz didn't care if she took it or not. "Those two are well on the way to hating each other."

"But they both care about you." Naomi hugged her. "Steve loves you. You're his mom. Eventually he'll help work this out."

I hope so. But as Liz recalled the retreating backs of both men, clouds engulfed the sun's warmth. She shivered in the gathering gloom.

7

"It's a good thing I won't have to leave town again until after our wedding." Jackson's hand, reaching across the Amishland Restaurant table, closed around Liz's cold fingers. "I missed you."

"It was only overnight, but I missed you too." What a difference his strong, sane presence made. She squeezed his hand, not minding the "Lord bless 'em" looks aimed their way. "I'm glad you're back."

She wasn't surprised that Jackson already knew about her Sweet Everything conversation with Geoffrey. "When I stopped for gas, Darla filled me in," he explained.

Their favorite convenience store clerk. "I suppose Darla wanted to make sure you heard the right version."

"Didn't want any suspicious old biddies to mess with our getting married," he said with a grin.

When she told Jackson about her son's dislike of Geoffrey, her fiancé expressed every confidence in Steve, just as Naomi had. "He's a great guy, Liz. He's just looking out for his mom."

Their server, Nadine, joked as she laid their bill by Jackson's plate. "You'll bring Liz here after you get married, won't you, Mayor? Otherwise, you'll be in big trouble with us."

He cringed in mock terror. "Wouldn't want that."

Their banter faded when Nadine described a customer who recently had asked her about the Olde Amish Inn. "It was an elderly lady with gray hair that seemed almost lavender. Nice clothes and real friendly."

A would-be guest? "What did she say?"

"Wanted to know how long you'd been in business and what

your bed-and-breakfast was like. She was thinking about taking some quilting lessons." The server winced. "I probably shouldn't have, but I told her you and Mayor Cross were getting married this month, and what a sweet couple you made."

"Well, *everybody* knows that." Jackson said with a wink.

Liz laughed. "Everything you told her is certainly public knowledge. Was she with someone?"

The server shook her head. "We were slow, so I spent extra time with her. She seemed real excited about your wedding."

"She's probably a sentimental old lady who likes to hear local gossip."

Nadine relaxed. "I'm glad I didn't open my big mouth when I shouldn't have."

"Not at all. I'm sure you made her evening."

Walking to his truck, though, Jackson said, "Probably harmless. Still, I'm not sure I like some stranger asking about you."

"If she had a gang tattoo, I might worry." Liz shrugged. "Actually, Nadine may have given me and Sew Welcome great PR. Perhaps she'll bring her ladies' circle for a retreat this fall."

Soon she'd kidded him out of his overprotectiveness, just as he'd helped her climb out of her Steve-versus-Geoffrey funk. But Jackson needed her perspective too. They balanced each other—exactly as they should.

Liz settled into his truck's comfortable leather seat with a contented sigh. Tonight's "marriage practice" had gone well.

Glancing at his handsome profile against the starry sky, she couldn't wait for the real deal.

After breakfast, Geoffrey made himself scarce, for which Liz was thankful. The Pembrokes and the Hensons checked out, then left to wander festivals in neighboring towns. After a refreshing service at her church, Pleasant Creek Community, Liz went to dinner with Mary Ann and Sadie.

Returning to her empty inn, Liz researched Bass Hollow's Trinity United Methodist Church, which didn't appear on the denomination's website. Liz did find a newspaper feature covering the church's recent closure because only three elderly members remained: Lettie and Alvin Starks and his cousin, John Engle. Lettie's obituary confirmed she'd passed away soon after, but Liz saw no indication the men had died. However, their contact information didn't appear in the usual Internet directories. Liz found a senior center in the next sizable town, Loganville. If she called after the holiday, perhaps someone could connect her with Alvin or John.

Enough research. Liz closed her laptop and dozed off in the breezy four-season room.

Steve's knock at the back door woke her.

He sat in a cushy rattan chair at her invitation, but his hands clenched and unclenched. "Mom, Geoffrey Teal is up to no good."

"How do you know?" Barely in time, Liz caught herself crossing her arms and made an effort not to. Steve was her son, not an opponent. "What, exactly, is his crime?"

"Well, none that we know of. Yet."

"So you think we should assume a person's guilt without concrete evidence?" Sometimes Liz's lawyer voice exerted more impact on Steve than her mom voice.

"You know I don't. But I don't ignore my instincts, either—instincts I learned to trust in the military."

She fidgeted. Now a young adult with extensive life experience, Steve and his impressions couldn't be discounted.

On the other hand, no matter her degrees or experience, no matter how many mysteries she'd solved, he still saw her as his mom. Carefully, she told Steve how Geoffrey's facts had matched hers.

Her son raised an eyebrow. "Okay, I'll grant that a fire destroyed your dad's adoption records, since you documented it. But that's awfully convenient. I think Geoffrey's using the absence of those records to weasel his way into your life."

Liz stared. "Why would he do that?"

"I don't know. Maybe to get a free place to stay. Maybe this is an ongoing con—victimizing innkeepers."

Liz chuckled mirthlessly. "I'm glad you think I'm so nice. But for your information, Geoffrey is paying for his room like any other guest."

"For now. What if he's working on you for a long-term arrangement?"

With difficulty, she summoned a wry smile. "I didn't know you thought I was such a pushover."

"You're not a pushover. Except when it involves family. Posers sense that in a second." Steve dropped his gaze and stared at his hands. "Mom, I don't want to insult you, but I'm sure this Geoffrey guy is a professional con man. He oozes charisma. Especially when he deals with women."

Liz counted to ten. "Hon, I dealt with all kinds in Boston. I've dealt with all kinds in Indiana." She leaned forward and patted his hand. "I appreciate your concern, but I want to find out if Geoffrey's claims are true. If they are, you and I have gained an uncle. If not—"she hardened her tone—"I'll sic Chief Houghton on him."

"Okay." Steve's tone didn't agree with his answer. He stood, planted a hasty kiss on her cheek, and left.

Liz watched his tall figure stride toward the lake. Should she follow? Sighing, she sat again. At this point, further discussion wouldn't accomplish anything.

What had Geoffrey done to press Steve's buttons? Her son hadn't balked when she had moved to Indiana and discovered her Amish family, and he'd been delighted when she and Jackson became engaged. Why was Steve so opposed to the possibility that Geoffrey might be her uncle?

Granted, the musician seemingly had popped out of nowhere. But why couldn't she and Steve handle this situation with their usual common sense?

Liz tried to recover her quiet afternoon, but within two minutes, Geoffrey poked his head through the door.

She sat up. For a moment, neither said anything.

Geoffrey ventured, "I had just pulled into the parking lot when I saw Steve headed here. That didn't go well, I take it?"

"You got that right."

He came in and sat near her. "I never meant to cause you problems, Liz. I suppose I should have thought of that before dropping a bomb on you—and Steve."

Yet how could Geoffrey have eased this surprise? Recalling Steve's remarks about the musician's alleged mooching, Liz flinched.

As if he'd read her mind, Geoffrey said, "My presence here is making things tough for you. So I've lined up a room in those extended-stay apartments on the outskirts of town, starting tonight. I'll be in number 205."

Liz coughed to cover her sigh of relief. "I wish I could change Steve's attitude, Geoffrey. But your moving out probably will help defuse the situation." If anything could. "I'll refund tonight's charges."

He shook his head. "No need. Call it my farewell present to you—though I still plan to be around for a few days," he said hastily. "And I'd like to come back."

Geoffrey's pensiveness, like a small boy's, caught in her throat.

"Whether you and Jackson invite me to your wedding or not, I'd love to share your special time."

She'd tried to avoid thinking about that scenario—walking down the church aisle on Steve's arm while Steve glowered at Geoffrey. Liz took a deep breath. "We haven't discussed it. But I'd like to see you again, Geoffrey." Her heart still hungered for her father, for some connection to him. Besides, she'd grown to like Geoffrey for himself. Liz pushed her son's crack about the musician's charisma aside. "Give Steve time to think. Call me in a day or two." By then, perhaps, she could have investigated more of his background.

His face brightened. "I'll do that."

He didn't stand in preparation to leave, so she did. Liz went to the kitchen, fished poppy seed bread from her freezer, and brought him the solid loaf. "Thanks for understanding, Geoffrey. I hope to see you soon."

"I hope so too. This bread will be gone in no time, you know." Grinning, he took it, fetched his bags, and waved goodbye as he headed out the door.

She thought of walking along the lake path, but she might encounter Steve again. If she walked downtown, she might run into Geoffrey.

Liz couldn't handle another session with either tonight.

Thump! Ring!

Liz smothered a laugh at the carny who oversaw the Muscle Man and His Hammer game at Wildton's Labor Day Festival. He gaped as Jackson, perspiration dripping, swung the heavy hammer six times in rapid succession, ringing the bell at the top without a miss.

"Man, you are one strong dude." The carny waved a calloused hand at rows of prizes in his booth. "Have your pretty lady pick something, anything."

A stuffed yellow octopus wouldn't enhance her decor, but its cute embroidered grin won Liz over.

"I'll cherish Oliver forever," she teased Jackson as they walked away.

"You'd better. I worked hard enough for him."

"You need a lemon slush." She stopped at a food stand and bought two.

As they walked and sipped, Jackson eyed several stands focused on beer sales. "Glad our town council voted no to alcohol at festivals. Changes the atmosphere, especially at night." His frown deepened. "Wish our fire station booth wasn't running short on help. After I leave, you and the Girls stick together, okay?"

How easily he forgot that she had made her own way in Boston for decades before coming to Pleasant Creek. Liz patted the hand that held hers. "Sadie will be with us, remember?"

"That's supposed to make me feel better?"

Liz laughed. Her earlier relaxation remedy had worked. She had mostly expunged yesterday's scene with Steve by taking a long drive this morning, listening to music. "Love, You Are My Friend" had lilted through her Acura more than once.

She and Jackson had enjoyed a carefree afternoon. Now they scanned rows of stands, trying to decide where to eat. Though fewer Amish vendors set up booths at Wildton festivals, delicious food was still available in plenty. Jackson filled up on all-you-can-eat fried fish at one stand. Liz thoroughly enjoyed a sausage, pepper, and onion sandwich from a neighboring stall. Elephant ears with decadent chocolate sauce and whipped cream finished their festival feast.

Groaning and holding their stomachs, they walked toward the vintage merry-go-round, where they were to meet the other Material Girls.

Jackson motioned toward the ticket booth. "Want a ride?"

The carousel, with its lights, mirrors, and multicolored ponies, brought back long-ago memories of riding gaudy, gallant horses with her laughing mother.

But her full stomach advised against it. “I don’t think so.”

“Me either,” Jackson admitted. “Maybe next year.”

Next year at this time, they would be anticipating their first anniversary. Jackson’s thoughts must have followed the same path, because his arm tightened around her. “We’ll do lots of fun things together between now and then.”

An earsplitting whistle nearly deafened them.

“Here we are!” Sadie’s unnecessary declaration drew the eyes of everyone around them. “Let go of our girl, Mr. Mayor, so she can come with us to the balloon show.”

Reluctantly Liz complied. Though a girls’ night out sounded fun, she wished she could share Wildton’s hot-air balloon display with Jackson.

“Call me when you get home.” He took Oliver the Octopus so Liz wouldn’t have to carry him, kissed her goodbye, and plunged into the crowd.

Naomi hugged her. “So glad we could all be off work tonight.”

She’d closed her bakery early because most Pleasant Creek inhabitants were enjoying parties and other nearby festivals. Mary Ann and Sadie had closed Sew Welcome for the holiday. Caitlyn had managed to get the day off, and even Opal had skipped her nonessential farm duties, leaving her husband, George, to do the rest.

Liz grinned. Labor Day hadn’t inspired much work.

As they walked the midway, they ran into several Pleasant Creek friends. To Liz’s surprise, they also encountered Vanessa.

“A customer in Huntington wanted to meet with me tomorrow, so I scheduled another quilting lesson with Miriam today. Your cousin’s wonderfully patient. And I loved visiting their farm,” Vanessa bubbled. “So peaceful.”

Then Miriam must have labored plenty. Remembering Vanessa’s terrible sewing, Liz hoped the lesson hadn’t lasted all day.

They invited her to join them, but Vanessa said she was meeting an old friend. In the meantime, other business opportunities had materialized in the Huntington area. "Liz, do you think after I'm finished—toward the end of the week—I could stay overnight with you on the way back to Lansing?"

"I'm sure at least one room will be available."

Vanessa promised to call once she knew more about her schedule. She waved goodbye, then wandered off to find her friend.

Liz and the Girls played more carnival games, then headed for what had been heralded as "The Great American Balloon Glow" in the festival's brochure. First, the colorful grounded balloons brightened and faded, forming dozens of different light patterns as their pilots alternately fed the flames in their baskets. Then one by one, each rose into the night sky with a *whoosh* to hover at different heights. Neon glow-in-the-dark tethers dangled from each balloon. Helpers on the ground grasped the tethers to prevent the balloons' escape.

The night sky resembled an inky ocean chock-full of brilliant jellyfish.

Liz joined the crowd in collective murmurs of awe, her spirits rising to float with the balloons, far above the hassles that had dragged her down lately.

Her mood still soared above the inn's gables as she unlocked the inn's front door and entered. She bent and hugged Beans, who grumbled under his breath at being disturbed from his slumber.

"You can't bring me down tonight, you old killjoy." He'd forgive her if she gave him a good scratch behind the ears.

Liz unlocked the door to her quarters, pushed it open, and automatically flicked on a light. *Eww!*

What appeared to have been an ice cream cake had melted all over her table and dripped to form a goopy puddle on the floor.

But the mess only held her gaze for a few seconds.

Across her living room, near the window and the lovely castor bean plant Geoffrey had given her, a body stretched across the floor like something from her nightmares.

It was Steve.

8

In the predawn hours, Steve lay stiff, a big mannequin in the hospital bed. Stan had said the burglar, probably hiding in the bathroom, must have stunned him with heavy blows from behind, then finished the attack with an additional blow to his face. How the assailant had gotten the drop on Steve, a trained military man, was unknown.

Right now, Liz wouldn't waste thoughts or feelings on the person who'd done this. She could concentrate only on her son's bruised cheek. The doctors weren't yet sure whether his eye would suffer permanent damage or whether he would need facial surgery. But that wasn't Steve's worst injury.

No, what the doctors were most concerned about was that he hadn't yet gained consciousness.

She said to Jackson, "The doctor said Steve should wake up soon."

"I'm sure he will." Her fiancé squeezed her hand. "He's one tough guy."

They'd repeated the same script several times during their vigil.

Steve, who had participated in special ops missions overseas, had completed them all mostly unscathed. Liz had to believe he couldn't just lie there much longer, purple-faced and helpless with a blood-stained bandage swathing his head. He would wake up. He *had* to.

Liz gripped her son's fingers, trying not to think of their last stressful encounter. Steve must have come to apologize. Her son had a key and had let himself in, ostensibly to surprise her. Instead, he'd surprised a burglar. Stan hadn't found anything in her quarters that had served as the intruder's weapon, so the chief had hypothesized that he'd brought a lead pipe or crowbar with him.

Liz couldn't have cared less about the details. All she cared about was Steve waking up.

"Hey, guys. I brought you breakfast."

Liz jumped. It was amazing how much older and in charge Caitlyn looked when she wore blue hospital scrubs. Her red-streaked hair and the butterfly tattoo on her neck didn't diminish the competence she exuded. She'd quietly managed the crazy flurry of police and friends, doing everything she could to guard her patient and maximize Liz's privacy.

Now the fragrance of bacon and eggs, mixed with pungent medical odors, rolled Liz's stomach. Jackson took a giant bite of his croissant sandwich, but Liz set hers on Steve's bedside table.

"No, don't put it there." Caitlyn picked up the sandwich. "Unwrap it."

"Okay." Liz turned back to check Steve's face. Had his eyelids fluttered?

"Come on, Liz," Jackson coaxed. "You need to eat."

"I'm not hungry."

"Maybe not." Caitlyn's hands went to her hips. "But Steve needs you to be strong and clearheaded. That won't happen if you don't take care of yourself."

To satisfy them, Liz unwrapped and nibbled the croissant. "Anybody ever tell you you're bossy?"

"Every day." Caitlyn shrugged, smiling. "Number one requirement in my job description."

Her arm briefly encircled Liz's shoulders. Liz paused to absorb the warmth. And to search her son's mottled face again.

"You know the Girls and I are here for you, Liz. And your family would camp here too, if I let them."

Only when Caitlyn barred the entrance had Miriam, Liz's aunt Ruth, and the other Material Girls gone home.

"I'll bet half the town is praying for Steve already," Jackson said. "The Pleasant Creek prayer chain never sleeps, you know."

"I know." She coaxed a smile to her lips. "Fortunately, God doesn't either." She raised her chin. "I am blessed. Steve is blessed. We'll make it."

Scooting his chair closer, Jackson clasped her to him in an embrace that was somehow comforting in spite of the awkward angle.

Why didn't hospitals include love seats in patient rooms? People needed to feel close, to hear each other's heartbeats. She eyed Steve's heart monitor.

He was looking at her!

"Steve!" Liz jumped to her feet and reached for his cheek, halting her hand midair when she remembered his injuries. Instead, she touched his shoulder, which was covered by the flimsy hospital gown.

Steve peered at her as if through a fog. His hand grasped hers as it had when he was a child, but he demanded answers as if she were an inept recruit. "Mom? You're all blurry. Where am I? What happened?"

Hours after Steve's incoherent awakening, laden with intense emotions that ranged from confusion to anger, he finally fell back asleep.

Jackson had brought Liz her laptop, then hurried off to his furniture factory to handle urgent matters.

Staring outside at the September sunshine, Liz was seized with a desire to call Geoffrey.

Odd. She hadn't yet determined whether he was family. Had she bonded with him more than she'd thought? Or was she suspicious of him? *Someone* had done this to Steve, and it was no secret they weren't exactly friendly. After arguing with herself, she walked into the hall and called Geoffrey. She only got his voice mail and left a message.

Next, to keep herself busy, she called the Tennessee United Methodist Church headquarters. The woman who answered clicked her tongue when Liz mentioned the Bass Hollow church. "I'm sorry, but their records were kept sporadically at best. I have no record of your father's baptism."

Maybe the Loganville senior center would link her to Alvin Starks or John Engle. This time, her contact knew both.

However, she hit another dead end. "I'm afraid they can't tell you anything about the church. Both Al and John are in a nursing home. They can't even remember their names."

Another roadblock. Liz returned to Steve's bedside and worked on her laptop, trying to forget the doctor's cautious prognosis.

Dr. Sam Schneider, who had delayed the chief's questioning Steve, said his blurred vision and erratic behavior and speech weren't unusual for someone with a moderate to severe head injury. His waking up was a positive sign, as he could have remained unconscious indefinitely. However, Steve remembered nothing from the past few days—certainly nothing about his attacker. Every five or ten minutes, he had demanded to know what had happened, then had immediately forgotten Liz's repeated replies.

As thankful as she was for Steve's awakening, Liz now clung to the quiet.

She opened her laptop. Though she didn't enjoy working with columns of numbers, they were consistent, predictable.

Though this time, her bank balance bounced off Liz like a dodgeball. Instead of finding less than she expected in the online bank report, Liz found more. Examining her deposits, she discovered a recent one for $3,000. Try as she might, she couldn't remember making it.

It was a problem most people would love, but right now, it only compounded the craziness.

There had to be an explanation. The deposit had been made the day Geoffrey had revealed their possible kinship. Had her distracted mind blanked on recording a regular transaction? But her guest income figures did not corroborate an extra $3,000!

She was still poring over spreadsheets when the chief appeared, bringing her coffee from Sweet Everything. "You look like you could use something better than vending-machine stuff."

"How right you are." After saving her work, she savored a large swallow. "I found something odd today in my accounts, a problem I've never had before."

"What's that?"

"An extra three grand."

The chief's eyes widened. "You call that a problem?"

"Well, with the roof repair costs higher than expected, I can certainly use it. Still, I'd like to know exactly where this extra money came from. It makes me paranoid to see a deposit on my statement that I can't recall." *That and other complications, such as a burglary and assault on my son.* Liz tried to laugh. "I've probably made a bad math mistake or had an early senior moment. If I can't figure it out, I'll check with Barb at the bank."

She hadn't meant to babble on about the discrepancy. Her mother had taught her that finances were strictly family matters.

As if he sensed her embarrassment, Stan gestured toward Steve. "I heard the good news."

His smile lifted her weary spirits. "It *is* good news. But Dr. Sam said no one could question Steve for at least another day."

"I didn't plan to." The chief patted her shoulder with his warm, calloused hand. "I was hoping to ask you a few questions. And to find out what's missing in your quarters."

"I haven't even thought about that." Wow. Maybe she *had* messed up the numbers and forgotten the deposit.

"You've had a lot on your mind." He gestured toward Steve, then asked about recent guests, repairmen, and others who might have gained access to the inn. Had she purchased any new valuables, such as antiques, that might have attracted thieves? "News gets around town, you know."

Yes, she knew. She'd learned in the past few years that privacy was an urban luxury.

"I know you don't want to leave Steve, but the sooner you find out what's missing, the better. Mary Ann and Sadie already have gone through their shop. The perp didn't tamper with anything there." The chief downed the last gulp of his own coffee. "Mary Ann said she'd stay with Steve while you check things out."

He tilted his head, examining her with kind eyes. "I'll bet you could use some rest. If you plan to stay here tonight, why don't you grab a nap after you look things over at the inn?"

"Maybe." She glanced at Steve's face, relaxed in almost childlike peace. Sleeping in her own bed sounded amazing, but could she nap in her quarters without wondering if his attacker would return to the scene of the crime? Or worse, to the hospital to make sure Steve couldn't tell anyone about what had happened?

Mary Ann popped in with her reassuring smile, and Liz rode with the chief to her home. She stopped short at the sight of yellow crime scene tape across her door.

The chief quickly removed it and handed her rubber gloves. "We've already processed the scene, but wear these just in case."

I have to do this again? She donned them numbly and turned the knob.

She made a surreal tour of the familiar. "So the burglar entered through this window."

It was obscured from street view by several shrubs.

The chief nodded. "Cut a small hole in the glass, unlocked, then opened it."

"More efficient this time, wasn't he?" Liz shifted wall panels to check her safe. As before, everything looked untouched. After an extensive search, she told the chief that nothing appeared missing from drawers or closets. Still, an unsettled feeling niggled at her as she surveyed her bedroom one more time.

Stan said, "Steve must have surprised him before he could take anything."

"At least, anything in here." Liz gestured toward the door to her quarters. "Most of my more valuable antiques are scattered throughout the inn."

The chief's quiet cough brought her back to the present. "Ready to check out the rest of the place?"

Liz nodded, but paused at the bedroom door.

"Something wrong?" His eyebrows hunched together.

"I . . . don't know."

"Take your time. I'll be in the rotunda." Stan left.

Feeling a little foolish, Liz surveyed the room again. The closet, dresser, and bed all looked normal. She didn't keep anything under her bed except the occasional dust bunny. A lamp and her Bible rested on the bedside table next to—

Liz blinked.

Her uneasiness finally zeroed in on the bare spot on the table.

Mom's diary.

Liz's mouth went dry. She'd sometimes carried it in her purse, but recently, she'd left it on the table so she could study a few pages whenever leisure permitted. She hadn't taken it out of her quarters.

Had she?

Liz conducted a fruitless search of her quarters, then told the chief about the missing journal. Together, they combed the inn.

Liz tried to focus on the possibility of other missing items, but they shrank in importance as she and the chief examined each room.

Especially now with her approaching wedding, Liz had clung to every curve of her mother's handwriting. But after scouring the inn and even her car, Liz sank into the rocker in the sitting room.

The diary was gone.

"Any idea why somebody would steal it?" Stan pushed back his thinning gray hair in a rare display of confusion.

Holding her mother's baby quilt as she rocked, Liz shook her head. She didn't know. But she would find out.

9

Liz had called Geoffrey no fewer than ten times since Steve's attack. His voice mail was full.

Had he turned off his phone? For someone who'd wanted to stay in close touch, he certainly was making himself scarce. She tried to cling to annoyance, but tiny fears pricked her thoughts.

They vanished temporarily when Jackson called, promising to spend a long noon hour with her and Steve. What a guy—so faithful, a rock amid chaos. He'd also collaborated more with the contractors, relieving her mind of that worry. The Materials Girls had been wonderful too, answering the inn's landline and tending to any business that arose.

The guests who had reserved rooms that weekend had proved understanding. They even rescheduled their getaways because they'd heard the Olde Mansion Inn was worth waiting for.

For the hundredth time, she prayed Steve would recover from the concussion that still scrambled his moods and his words.

Liz glanced at her son, snoozing peacefully after another confused, angry night. She pushed back a strand of hair from her face. She must look like a complete mess. A long, hot bath at home sounded so good. Maybe she could slip in another nap. Even one hour's solid sleep might bring her back to life.

Caitlyn breezed into the room. "How's it going, Liz?"

Though Caitlyn also had tended to Steve—as well as other difficult patients—throughout the night, she surveyed him with bright, alert eyes. "I know last night wasn't fun, but Dr. Sam was pleased that his vision's improving."

"Yes, thank goodness for that." The eye surgeon their family doctor had called in hadn't detected any major damage to Steve's eye, and the blurriness had diminished somewhat. "I'm still waiting to hear from the plastic surgeon whether Steve will need surgery on his cheekbone. But Dr. Sam seems to think that this brain bruise—that's what he called it—will resolve in a few weeks."

"Just in time for your wedding." Caitlyn's smile coaxed Liz's out of hiding.

Wobbly hopes rose inside her. "Steve might even come home in a couple of days."

"Exactly. He's improving, so you certainly can take a few hours off." Caitlyn clasped Liz's hands, raised her from the chair, and took her place. "I'm off shift now, so I can stay with Steve while you go home." She grinned. "Trust me, if he wakes up, I'll make him behave."

"I believe it." Caitlyn had managed Steve's moods better than Liz. She left with only a twinge of anxiety.

On her way home, Liz turned toward Geoffrey's apartment. If he'd been performing at late-night gigs, he might be sleeping. *Too bad.* He should have called her back.

She climbed the bare stairs to the second floor of the slightly musty building and rapped on number 205's door. No answer. She pounded.

A voice behind her made her jump, but it wasn't Geoffrey's.

"Sorry to scare you," Stan's grimace told Liz he wasn't particularly glad to see her.

Why was he here? "Have you seen Geoffrey? Heard from him?"

"I was hoping you had. I've talked to your other guests, and they panned out—though, I have to say, those Pembroke ladies were a double headache."

Liz suppressed a grin. Yes, she could imagine the Pembrokes had complicated his day.

"But I've come here twice before at different times to talk to your maybe uncle. Thought I'd try this morning, but no dice, right?"

"So it appears. I haven't seen or heard from Geoffrey since he moved here." The prickles of her earlier uneasiness now jabbed her insides. Did his lack of communication have anything to do with the attack on Steve?

"Maybe Mrs. Beck's seen him."

Liz had heard that the older lady manager not only lived there, but kept careful track of her tenants' comings and goings. The chief didn't invite Liz to accompany him, but she followed him to the woman's basement apartment anyway.

"Nope, haven't seen hide nor hair of him for days." Mrs. Beck's sharp blue eyes flicked from the chief to Liz. "What's he done?"

"No evidence he's done anything," Stan said. "Just wanted to ask him a few questions and make sure he's all right."

Mrs. Beck harrumphed. "Of course, he's all right. But he's got himself into trouble, hasn't he?" She muttered, "Too good-looking for his own good."

Despite her concern, Liz couldn't help smiling.

The chief continued, "Would you let us into his apartment for a few minutes?"

The old woman grumbled, but took a large ring of keys from a nail and led the way back to apartment 205.

Though the chief said he didn't expect trouble, he cautioned both Liz and Mrs. Beck to stand a short distance down the hallway, then positioned himself beside the door and hammered it. "Police! Open up, Teal!"

When no one answered, Stan turned the key and pushed the door open.

Even from a distance, Liz could see the apartment's front room looked bare as if it had been unoccupied for months.

Mrs. Beck exploded. "I knew he was a bad 'un! He's skipped out on me!"

Though the chief's eyes had hardened, he said evenly, "Let's not assume that yet. I'll look around to make sure."

Liz ached to follow him into the apartment, but she knew better. The backdrop of Mrs. Beck's acidic narrative made their hallway vigil even less bearable. Fists—and heart—clenched, Liz conceded that the manager and Steve were probably right. Maybe Geoffrey had disappeared because he'd assaulted her son and stolen her diary, though she couldn't imagine why. Or why Geoffrey would have conned her into thinking they were kin.

But something told her he was in danger.

Liz tried to shake it off. Geoffrey had emptied his apartment. She should empty her concern. At the very least, Geoffrey had ignored her when she'd needed him most. *Some family.*

Finally, a granite-faced Stan emerged and told them Geoffrey appeared to have abandoned his apartment in a hurry. "He left a camp chair, card table, disposable dishes, and some food in the fridge. Took his clothes and personal effects, though. I didn't find guitars or music."

Liz closed her eyes, trying to blot out her mental video of a smiling Geoffrey playing for coffee hour. No, Geoffrey wouldn't have left his music behind.

"Doesn't sound like too much of a mess," Mrs. Beck said grudgingly, "and he did pay a full month's rent."

"Give Teal a few days. Maybe he'll come back," the chief said.

You don't believe that. Liz didn't either.

Despite Mrs. Beck's superior track record of nosiness, she knew nothing about Geoffrey's performance schedule. "I heard him come in real late, but didn't see him during the day."

"I don't know about his gigs either," Liz agreed, "but surely we can check entertainment sites and find out where he's playing this week. I can at least do a search on his name." She pulled out her phone. Stan did likewise.

Mrs. Beck scowled. "I hate them things! Fancified phones will be the ruination of the whole country."

"Might be," the chief agreed. "But lock this door, will you? Let me know if Teal shows up. And don't let anybody into his apartment without talking to me."

Muttering, she complied, then stomped toward the stairs, keys jingling.

Liz called, "Goodbye, Mrs. Beck."

The woman disappeared into the basement.

"Just as well that she's not hanging around. The grapevine will know way too much as it is." The chief frowned at his phone. "Teal doesn't have a criminal record in Indiana's database. But he's from Tennessee, right?"

"Nashville." Liz frowned too. "Maybe if I check those local entertainment and event sites, Geoffrey's name might be listed. But at the moment, I can't find him."

Stan said quietly, "Maybe you won't ever find him, under that name, anyway."

Liz tried to swallow the angry wad of worry in her throat. "You think he's connected somehow with stealing my diary? With attacking Steve?"

"I'm not sure what to think—at least, not until I talk to the police in Nashville. I can get away with entering Teal's apartment to check on his safety, but to consider it a crime scene, I'll need a warrant." He turned a piercing gaze on her. "Not that I want you to go looking for evidence, Liz. Stay away from this one."

She glared back. "When this case involves a man who claimed to be *my* father's brother? When *my* mother's diary was stolen? When *my* son was assaulted?"

Stan's official expression gave way to a fatherly look that only irritated her more. "That's exactly why I don't want you to look for Teal. You've got Steve to take care of. And you're right—every point of this case could blow you sky-high. You'd try to be objective, but that would be impossible. Right?"

She yanked her gaze away from his knowing one.

"This guy might be more dangerous than we think. Why ask for more trouble, especially when you're getting married soon? It's a special time for you and Jackson. He'd like things to stay nice and uncomplicated for a change, wouldn't he?"

That was playing dirty, especially since it was true.

Liz left. After escaping the building, she dropped into her Acura's front seat. She couldn't just do nothing. It went against every fiber of her being.

As much as she loved Steve, Liz could hardly bear sitting in his hospital room, hour after hour, unable to help him—while the man who had injured him walked around scot-free. If that man was Geoffrey Teal, she wouldn't rest until she dragged him to jail herself.

She didn't want the ludicrous mental picture to lessen her anger, but it did. Annoying thoughts of delaying action until she could think rationally darted through her mind—

Out of the corner of her eye, she saw the bank, solid and reassuring despite its whimsical Swiss-chalet appearance, commonplace in Pleasant Creek. She hadn't had time to call Barb about the weird deposit, but now was the perfect time to deal with it. At least one disturbing issue could be resolved. Liz jumped out of the car and hurried toward the bank entrance.

When Liz explained her concern about the unknown deposit,

however, Barb's pleasant smile faded. "We found the cash in a plain white envelope in the night deposit box, with a note that it was to go into your account. I just assumed you'd run out of deposit slips."

Liz shook her head. "My brain's been scrambled lately, but I'd remember doing that." Especially as she'd never handled that much cash. "Wouldn't your security camera have caught the depositor on video?"

Barb promised to check the recording. "It's certainly an atypical situation. Mostly we work to protect customers from theft. I can't recall dealing with an anonymous gift."

Liz understood Barb's bemusement. Nevertheless, this shadowy benefactor's action added one more spoonful of unease to her life, which was full of more than enough of that at the moment.

"By the way," a conspiratorial tinge colored Barb's businesslike tone, "I heard from my aunt Hattie that your uncle seems to have disappeared."

How could the grapevine have discovered Geoffrey's absence so quickly?

Liz's mental blankness must have transferred to her face, because Barb added, "My aunt Hattie Beck. You know, Mrs. Beck, who manages the apartments?"

Oh.

"I check on her every day, and she always knows what's going on around town." Barb tutted. "Goodness, I hope your uncle's all right. Why, I saw him just yesterday morning, going into the library." She simpered like a teenager. "He is one handsome guy."

The library? Hadn't Geoffrey said that he hated to read? Liz said, "Thanks. We hope he just took a little trip and forgot to tell anyone."

She thanked Barb and waved goodbye. Exiting the bank, she made a beeline for the library, still puzzling about the manager's comment. Geoffrey had still been in town yesterday morning—the morning after Steve's assault. Knowing the police would want to question him, he must have left soon afterward. Yet a nonreader had taken time to go to the library?

Liz entered the beautiful old building and approached the circulation desk. As she'd hoped, Loretta Simmons, head librarian and another vital link in the Pleasant Creek grapevine, was busily cataloging new books.

"Why, yes, your uncle came in yesterday. Geoffrey Teal, right? Mary Ann told me all about him, and I'd seen him downtown. He was very nice, though he didn't stay long. I tried to find out what genre he likes to read so I could make recommendations, but he went downstairs to the reference area for a few minutes, then left."

Liz hurried downstairs before Loretta could pump her for more information about Geoffrey.

She'd often used the reference area when she'd first moved to Pleasant Creek. A quick review of the shelves revealed nothing new there. A full third of the basement was taken up by shelves, boxes, and piles of musty books and magazines. If Geoffrey was looking for a specific one, how would he ever find it? Liz promised herself she'd spend more time here later.

As she and the Acura approached her inn, its homey front porch begged her to stay. Though her quarters had been violated by the scum who had injured Steve, it still beckoned to her like an old friend.

Sadly, there was no time for a nap or a leisurely bath. But while she luxuriated in a hot shower, she pondered Geoffrey's library visit. Had he been looking for local information found only there? She sighed as she packed yogurt and fruit into an insulated bag in the kitchen, wondering how she could find more information on Geoffrey Teal. Liz gathered up a few other essentials and hurried back to the hospital.

"Hey, Liz." Caitlyn greeted her.

"Hi, Mom." Steve smiled crookedly, a first since the burglary.

Despite bruises and swelling, Liz caught a glimpse of his pre-injured self, and her traitorous eyes filled.

"I didn't mean to make you cry. I just said hi."

Liz brushed her tears aside with a shaky laugh. "I'm kind of crazy these days. But I'm so glad to see you're doing better. Caitlyn must be magic."

"I am," her friend said with a grin. "But I think Steve's up for some mom magic too."

Though upbeat, Steve seemed tired. When Liz encouraged him to sleep, he dropped off within minutes.

This time, she ignored her laptop's spreadsheets and escaped into a thriller whose heroine, by comparison, made Liz's life look easy. At noon, Jackson appeared as promised, and while Steve slept on and off, they enjoyed time together before Jackson returned to town hall.

After he left, Steve fell into a deep sleep. Unable to think of anything else to do for the case, Liz tried to return to her thriller, but when one more car bomb detonated in the story, she slapped it shut. She should have picked a more peaceful genre given her current state.

The late afternoon vigil sometimes proved as lonely as those during the wee hours, with Jackson gone and the Material Girls generally occupied until evening. Occasionally, Liz slipped into the hallway to walk and chat with the staff or other patients' relatives in the waiting room.

But Liz's mom instinct tethered her to Steve's side. Her weariness only heightened her edginess.

She remembered too well an overnight hospital stay after her car accident as a teen. Had her mother watched Liz's every breath too?

Yes, she remembered, each time she had awakened that restless, painful night, her mother's gaze had been locked on her—though Liz had been injured far less severely than Steve.

Remembering the deep love and rare anxiety in those gray eyes, Liz was seized with a hunger for her mother's touch.

In the past, when grief overtook her, she'd read her mother's diary, clutched it close to her heart, or simply carried it in her purse.

She couldn't do that now.

Ignoring hot, sour anger, Liz opened her laptop. The thief might have stolen her mom's diary, but Liz had saved the lyrics and given a copy to Jackson.

She read them several times, soaking in them like the warm bath she'd missed. Soon, though, renewed questions tugged her out of long-ago remembrances. With all that had happened recently, she hadn't thought much about the song. Now might be a great time to research it.

The lyrics popped up immediately, attributed to Trey Edmond, just as the DJs had said.

Hmm.

Liz hadn't heard any other song by that artist. She did a search on him as well.

She froze when she saw a photo of him.

With a trembling finger, she enlarged it.

The tall, blond singer was clean-shaven, showing off chiseled good looks.

Unlike Geoffrey, who had a brown mustache and beard.

But unless Geoffrey had a twin, he and Trey Edmond were one and the same.

10

Liz's overloaded mind had turned mushy like the hospital cafeteria's lukewarm oatmeal, and it didn't improve the next day.

Steve, however, was feeling somewhat better. He had graduated from hospital gown to flannel pants and a T-shirt. Because of lingering dizziness and nausea, the doctor only allowed him up for short amounts of time. Now Steve tossed and turned in the hospital bed, clearly restless and still occasionally disoriented. Dr. Sam said he might go home tomorrow, but today he needed more tests.

While that was happening, Liz exited and parked herself in the waiting room with laptop, phone, and a paper cup of watery vending-machine coffee. She automatically checked messages, texts, and e-mails. There was nothing from Geoffrey, despite her continued efforts to contact him.

Liz sighed and called Innovation Sounds, the Nashville company that had published "Love, You Are My Friend." Had Trey Edmond produced evidence that he'd written the song? A friendly young secretary assured Liz she'd soon hear from the appropriate person.

Next, Liz combed the Internet for any evidence that Geoffrey/Trey had told her anything that was true.

As she clicked and swiped, she tried to delete her mental slideshow of his stay at her inn: the gifts, the moment he'd told her he was her uncle, the effortless movement of his fingers on guitar strings, playing music that warmed her guests' coffee hour.

She gagged on the memory and the quickly cooling coffee in the cup. No wonder Geoffrey hadn't sung. They all would have recognized Trey Edmond's voice in a minute.

Was Geoffrey Teal the performer's real name? Had he lied about his entire history, including their kinship? She could hardly believe anyone could concoct such a convincing tale without some shred of truth. Though, if Geoffrey were an expert con man—Steve's crack about his appeal to women still burned her cheeks—he could sell it with accompanying fake certificates.

But why had he gone to such elaborate lengths to prove they were related? How did all these bizarre puzzle pieces fit?

She found a Geoffrey Teal in Nashville whose social media photos and information matched, but he could have faked those, as well as the certificates. Geoffrey's performance photos looked far less elaborate than Trey Edmond's. Geoffrey emphasized a simple country lifestyle. Trey gravitated toward glitz. Despite twin features and builds, the two couldn't seem more different.

That wasn't surprising if he had designed and assumed two identities to deceive her.

Liz moved on to the family tree Geoffrey had provided. She found several Jon Teals in Lexington, as well as a host of others with the same last name and a number of Anita Teals. As Liz worked her way through the list, her mind wandered back to the burglaries.

The first seemed almost half-hearted, as the intruder had ignored many expensive items that were available. That attempt at breaking into her quarters had failed.

The second burglary could have been unrelated. But assuming the same burglar had returned, the second break-in had made him guilty of a more serious crime and earned him no benefit except Liz's mother's diary.

Perhaps the diary had been the focus of both crimes?

That would fit the robber's haphazard thievery during the first event. Then, he wouldn't have found what he really sought, even if he'd managed to enter her quarters. Liz had been carrying the diary in her purse at that time.

Yet why would the intruder take double risks for an old journal? It had only contained her mother's memories.

And the song lyrics.

Liz's hands froze on the keyboard. The lyrics had existed long before Trey Edmond/Geoffrey Teal claimed to have written them. She'd realized that earlier. But she hadn't given much thought to the song's growing popularity. It was earning him not only fame, but probably big bucks, with the potential for much more.

Innovation Sounds was benefiting as well.

Did the company know that Trey Edmond had lied about his authorship? Or perhaps it was a conspiracy. Liz crushed her paper coffee cup and hurled it into a trash can.

Still, if Geoffrey were indeed the thief, why would he focus on Mom's diary? Yes, it proved his claims to authorship false. Surely, though, some other songbook or recording from the 1970s would prove an equal threat. Unless—unless—

Liz caught her breath.

Unless the diary was the only place the song could be found.

Unless the song had originated with her mother.

Liz's limp hands typed a line of gibberish, sending a bewildered search engine in half a dozen directions.

Slowly she closed the browser. But she couldn't close down impossible thoughts that pinged in her mind.

Liz's mother, an intelligent, down-to-earth woman, obviously had enjoyed recording daily life in her journal, but never wrote her own lyrics or poetry. On top of that, she sang every song, including the national anthem, using two notes that existed in no known musical scale.

Abigail Eckardt could not have written "Love, You Are My

Friend." Yet the words to the song were in her diary. Mom had even tried to sing it aloud.

"Liz! Liz!" The morning nurse's panic crashed through Liz's ponderings. "Come! Please!"

Liz leaped from the chair and dashed toward Steve's room. She saw Jackson sprinting from the other direction. He steered her inside, where Steve roared and thrashed while the petite nurse failed to quiet him.

"Steve! What's wrong?" Liz demanded.

"That—that—" Steve bellowed an epithet he'd never used in front of her and must have learned in the military.

"Calm down." Jackson's words cemented a barrier between them. He edged Liz to the side. "Tell us what's wrong in words your mother can actually be proud of you for using."

Steve spat out his words, "I heard somebody talking in the hall, saying the police are looking for Teal. I told you he was bad news, Mom. But you wouldn't listen."

She wanted to cover her face. "I'm so sorry—"

"He lied to you. He did this to me! That's why he skipped town!" Slinging the covers across the room, Steve flung himself out of bed and stormed toward the door, the little nurse clinging to him like a determined Yorkie.

Mid-stride, Steve swayed and the intact portion of his face paled.

"See? You're not up for barreling off in a rage. Lean on me." Jackson pushed his strong shoulder under Steve's arm, while Liz encircled his waist with her arm.

Together, they got Steve back to the bed. He flopped against the pillow, chest heaving.

A muscular orderly, summoned by the nurse, had appeared.

"Better not try that again," Jackson advised Steve. "Looks like they have a bodyguard on you now."

Steve closed his eyes, still panting.

Liz covered his hand with hers. She said quietly, "Maybe Geoffrey did play me for a fool. And if he hurt you, it makes me angrier than you can imagine."

At her tone, Steve's eyes popped open and his face crumpled. "I'm sorry, Mom." The near faint seemed to have drained the anger from him. "You, too, Jackson. And—and—" He waved a feeble hand toward the nurse and orderly, then let it drop. "It's just that Teal's out there, doing great, and I don't know if I'll ever be the same again. I'm just glad it wasn't you, Mom."

"You will be fine." Liz raised her chin. "Dr. Sam, the eye doctor, and now the plastic surgeon have all said that getting back to normal is just a matter of time. And taking care of yourself." She gave him a stern gaze.

She gestured to the hospital workers, and they slipped out of the room.

She turned back to Steve. "You should be fine in a few weeks. Dr. Sam's talking about your going home soon." Liz stuck her hands on her hips. "That is, if you don't pull a stunt like this again. Yes, blowups may occur because of your brain injury, but you do have some control over yourself. How can we get you well if you throw fits like this?"

A flush pinked his uninjured cheek. "I'll try to behave, Mom. Honest."

His slight, crooked grin reminded her of his penitent, middle-school self. "See that you do," she said, chuckling, though she was trying to be stern.

"Some women are cute when they're mad," Jackson told Steve conspiratorially before he left to return to work. "But your mom is downright scary."

Steve snorted. "You have no idea."

The Steve crisis had wiped her out. She thought longingly of stretching out on a waiting room sofa. But Steve had been asleep awhile and soon would awaken. Perhaps she was overdoing the "being there for you" thing, but she couldn't stomach his feeling alone, not even for a short time.

Liz called Innovation Sounds again. The secretary repeated her bright assurance that the appropriate person would call back as if it was recorded. Liz delved a little more into Geoffrey research, but had lost her appetite for it. And after Stan had discouraged—actually, forbidden—her to work on the case, should she tell him what she knew?

Her phone vibrated. It was Barb. She'd been waiting to hear from the bank. Suddenly awake, Liz slipped into the hallway. "Did you find anything on that security video?"

"Well, yes. A tall woman or medium-sized man—I couldn't tell which—wearing jeans and a very baggy hoodie deposited that cash. I couldn't see the face."

If only she could talk Stan into checking for fingerprints. "I assume your teller tossed the envelope and note at the time of the deposit?"

Barb's voice turned eager. "Yes, but I can give you the second note."

Liz said sharply, "What do you mean, the second note?"

"Well, your unknown benefactor has struck again."

Liz's jaw dropped.

"This time, whoever it was deposited $5,000."

11

"I'm meeting with a new customer and wanted to take another quilting lesson with Miriam. But when Mary Ann told me you'd been in the hospital, I had to see how you were doing."

Vanessa Leighton, who had joined in Steve's unofficial welcome-home party, clasped his hand as he relaxed on a sitting room sofa.

"Wow, thanks." He grinned, looking a little uncomfortable at all the attention. But as they chatted about Vanessa's latest letter from her soldier son, Steve appeared more like himself than he had in days.

After expressing her own gratitude for Vanessa's kindness, Liz sank into her rocker. She was so relieved to be home, even if things were crazy with all the Material Girls, plus Sarah and Miriam, competing to see who could wait on them the most.

"Vanessa's staying with me tonight," Sadie announced.

"I am?" Vanessa shot her a quizzical look. "Now that all Liz's other guests have checked out, I was going to stay at a motel so Liz wouldn't worry—"

"Forget that. Come over after you're done quilting. And I'm bringing you here for breakfast tomorrow. We're gonna make Steve's favorite—blueberry pancakes and lots of bacon."

Steve all but licked his chops. "Sounds awesome."

"That does sound like a great plan." After receiving directions from Sadie, Vanessa gave Miriam a ride back to her farm. The others, except for Opal, gradually scattered, and Steve, worn out from all the love, fell asleep.

"You catch a nap too. No excuses." Her prim friend eyed Liz sternly. "I'm here if he needs something, and I've already told Jackson to take you out for supper. You don't want to fall asleep with your face in your plate, do you?"

Not the romantic picture Liz wanted Jackson to hold in his heart forever. "I have to do business stuff first. But I'll sleep. I promise."

She took her laptop to the sun-dappled four-season room, and after taking care of reservations for the inn, she opened her financial program. For now, the $8,000 dollars remained in her bank account. So far, no witnesses to the depositor's late-night actions had surfaced. The chief had checked the second envelope for fingerprints, but no matches had turned up in Indiana's criminal database.

A person who gave, rather than took, wasn't a criminal anyway. Was he?

Liz closed the program, hoping a migraine, circling her head like a buzzard, wouldn't land. Liz checked her phone, but there was nothing from Geoffrey. Automatically, she tried again to contact him every way she knew.

He hadn't posted anything new on his blog this week, which was unlike him given the previous dates on it.

Liz noticed all of Trey Edmond's posts consisted of canned publicity information she'd seen before. Normally, he added a daily personal note.

Why had those disappeared the past few days?

Liz called Innovation Sounds again. When a cheerful male voice answered, she pretended to be a fan who had heard rumors that Trey Edmond had canceled his next concert. "Is he sick? I've been waiting ages to see him live!"

Sounding less pleasant than before, the man told Liz to disregard any rumors and continue to check their official website for accurate concert information. When she pressed for information about "Love,

You Are My Friend," he replied that the person in charge of that department would be gone the next two weeks.

Liz wanted to hurl her phone against the wall, but she didn't need a broken phone on top of everything else. Instead, she threw all five pillows off the sofa. Innovation Sounds seemed on a mission to keep her at bay indefinitely. Perhaps all music companies, having invested in musicians and their songs, evaded questions about songs' origins.

But her gut didn't buy it. Initially, her instinct had whispered that Geoffrey was in trouble. Now it shouted *danger!* But for him or for her?

She'd promised Opal that she'd sleep. Instead, the beginnings of a plan whirled in her mind.

Liz was going to Nashville.

Pancake number four was quickly followed by number five.

Liz lost count of the blueberry pancakes Steve had forked onto his plate. It was so good to see him eat with his usual enthusiasm. Caitlyn, sitting beside him, teased him into nonstop smiles.

Would he lose ground when Liz told him she was leaving for Nashville the next day—and the reason why she was going?

She wasn't doing justice to her own pancake. Jackson, with whom she had shared her plan at dinner the night before, knew why.

Soon the others noticed.

"Not going on a diet, are ya?" Sadie's new fall hat, bristling with little pumpkins and scarecrow faces, shook ominously. "Save it until tomorrow, when I'm not cooking."

"Hear, hear." Vanessa waved her fork. "Dieting's not allowed today."

"Mom, are you upset about something?" Steve *was* feeling better. The concern in his voice—more typical of his usual demeanor—made her stomach clench with guilt.

"A little," she admitted. "I suppose I should explain a few things to all of you, since we're together." Liz cast an apologetic glance at Vanessa. "You've shared in some of these, um, complications, so feel free to stay. But don't think you have to listen to all this."

Declaring herself to be their official dishwasher, Vanessa diplomatically collected plates and silverware, and then exited to the kitchen.

Liz told them about her discovery that Geoffrey was Trey Edmond.

She didn't want to meet Steve's gaze, but she had to.

His eyes glinted, but he said nothing.

"Of course!" Naomi slapped her forehead. "When Geoffrey played his guitar, something went *ding* in my head, but I didn't put two and two together."

"But is he your uncle?" Opal's keen eyes fixed on Liz.

She hesitated. "I haven't finished my research about his background, but his actions seem to imply that he isn't. First, he concealed the truth about his being Trey Edmond."

Caitlyn suggested, "Maybe he was having trouble getting used to being famous and just wanted his space."

"I could buy that," Liz agreed, "except that Geoffrey disappeared after the second burglary, which makes me—and Stan—think that he had something to do with it."

Sadie glowered. "I highly doubt it's coincidental."

"Especially if he took my mom's diary. And I've figured out a reason why he might do that." Liz told them her hypothesis about the song. "I couldn't understand how the song could originate with my mother, who never sang a song on key in her life, but now I think I've got that straight."

That realization during her long, restless night had warmed her weary heart. "I think my father wrote it."

A collective "Ohhh!" met Liz's words.

"He must have been an excellent musician," Mary Ann said.

"My dad majored in music in college. That particular song must have been special to Mom, to them. That's why she recorded the words in her diary and tried to sing it."

"And that's another reason we need Kiera to sing it at our wedding," Jackson added.

"Absolutely. And since your dad wrote it, he should receive credit as its composer," Mary Ann declared. "Not to mention that you, as his heir, should be receiving royalties from it."

"True. I can always use the money, but that's not the big issue." Liz tried to control the anger that wobbled her voice. "I need to know the truth. If Geoffrey attacked my son and stole my mom's diary *and* my dad's song, I need to report him to the authorities, even if we share some biological bond. And I definitely won't be chasing after any kind of relationship with my so-called 'uncle.'"

Silence. Steve leaned forward.

Liz's throat tightened so that she had to inhale another deep breath. "But I don't know anything for sure. I won't rest until I do."

She wasn't about to voice her fears that Geoffrey might be in danger. Instead, she told them how Innovation Sounds had stonewalled her. "I think they may hold answers to my questions. So I want to pay them a little visit. I'm leaving for Nashville tomorrow."

"*We* are leaving for Nashville tomorrow," Jackson corrected her.

She smiled at him, then said to the group, "I hope we can resolve some major issues Monday morning, then return that night." She hesitated. "You've all been wonderful, especially with Steve's injury, and I'll need your help to pull this off. As always."

"Of course." Sadie's emphatic nod shook the pumpkins on her hat. "I'm going with you."

"Um . . ." Liz exchanged glances with Jackson. To quiet the Pleasant

Creek grapevine, they'd thought of asking Mary Ann. But Sadie?

Their hesitancy didn't undermine her determination in the least. "You know you need me."

Sadie was right, Liz realized with a start. She was utterly fearless and resourceful. If anyone could help them get answers, it was Sadie.

Jackson must have experienced a similar epiphany, because they said together, "All right, Sadie."

"So, that's settled." Sadie aimed a thumb at Steve. "Caitlyn, you got him tomorrow night?"

"You bet." Caitlyn nodded her red head. "I'll drop by a couple of times to check on him—"

"How about staying for popcorn and a movie?" Steve had brightened.

"Sure. Then you can call me if you need anything overnight."

"Why don't I stay the night in my bakery's back room?" Naomi offered. "Being next door, I'll be available if you need immediate help."

"Thanks." Steve sounded as grateful as Liz felt.

Mary Ann turned to Liz. "I can keep an eye on the inn while you're gone."

"And if unexpected guests come, I'll help Sarah with them," Opal said. "If we need more help, I'll ask Miriam to lend a hand."

"You're all incredible," Liz whispered, overwhelmed.

Jackson nodded agreement. "What time are we leaving?"

Mary Ann invited the travelers, plus Steve, to Sunday dinner, after which they would head for Nashville. After nailing down a few more details, the group adjourned, Liz to the sparkling kitchen, where she found a note from Vanessa. Her new friend had left to meet with her customer, then would head back to Lansing.

And then I get to stay for two whole weeks! she'd written.

"I didn't thank her," Liz lamented as she and Jackson sat together in the four-season room.

"Maybe you can send her a discount on a night's stay," Jackson suggested with a smile.

Pleasant hours passed as they took advantage of the post-breakfast quiet—Steve was napping—and the beautiful weather outside. With Mary Ann and Sadie in their shop and her phone in her pocket, Liz felt confident enough to leave the inn for a leisurely stroll around the lake.

So glad we chose September. It was neither too hot nor too cool, with green trees embroidered with gilded, brilliant colors. Perhaps a giant harvest moon would make an appearance around their wedding date.

Because he'd spent so much time at the hospital, Jackson had to leave for work that Saturday. Liz checked on Steve, who assured her he was perfectly happy playing video games and reading all afternoon. "Better cure than all those pills they gave me in the hospital," he said with a grin. "But don't tell Caitlyn I said that. She'll come up with a bunch of new ones for me to take out of spite."

She laughed, both at his humor and with relief. Steve certainly had begun to act more like himself.

"I'm not sure why you have to do all this," he said now, his eye twinkles fading. "Though, at first, I guess I wanted to find Teal too." He scowled. "But now I'm glad he's gone. Let God deal with him." Steve's big arm enclosed her in a hug. "I just want you and Jackson to get married and be happy."

For the first time in days, the anvil-like heaviness on her shoulders had dissipated. Steve was improving, just as the doctor had said he would.

Liz moved through the inn, tying up her own loose ends and packing. When she returned from Nashville, she and the Material Girls should review reception details. She peeked at her wedding dress once more, visualizing Jackson's face as she walked down the aisle.

She was mentally decorating the church sanctuary when she

opened the front door to retrieve her mail. An enormous bouquet of white roses and lilies, punctuated by lovely greenery, greeted her.

Mary Ann and Sadie, locking up Sew Welcome, spotted her as she carried it in. They swooped across the rotunda, oohing and aahing.

Sadie needled Liz, "We'll see if Jackson sends flowers after a year."

"I think he will. That boy is *gone* on you." Mary Ann nodded confidently.

Liz set the flowers on the counter and opened the card.

Congratulations on your upcoming wedding.

There was no signature.

"You better read it to us, or I will." Sadie made a playful swipe at the card.

Mary Ann cocked her head. "Is something wrong, dear?"

"I'm not sure." Liz handed her the card.

Mary Ann's forehead crinkled.

"Let me see too." Looking over Mary Ann's shoulder, Sadie's mischievous grin faded.

Liz said, "Well, someone is very . . . thoughtful."

Sadie snorted. "Who does that?"

"I wish I knew." Liz ran her fingers through her hair. "There's nothing threatening about the flowers or card that I can see."

"No poison ivy or anything," Sadie agreed.

"Still, there's just something off about this." Mary Ann pulled Liz away from the bouquet. "Given all that's happened lately, I'd tell Stan about it. And Jackson."

First, Liz called the town florist, who assured her that she hadn't filled the order.

The bouquet puzzled the chief as well. "Odd. But after all, you are marrying the mayor, Liz. Some sweet old lady who's just too shy to meet you or give her name might have left the flowers."

"I've had worse surprises," Liz said truthfully. "Still, there's something strange about this."

"If it bothers you, toss it. And keep an eye out for anything else that seems out of line."

Jackson was more forthright. "Throw a bag over those flowers and pitch them, Liz. With the burglaries and Steve's getting hurt, even a suggestion that something's weird should raise red flags."

"You're right." She sighed. "But they're so beautiful that it seems a shame."

His voice softened. "You never know when a good surprise or two might be in store over the next few weeks."

Replaying that sentence in her mind made it easier to take the flowers to the trash. But their ghost lingered in her thoughts, and Liz found herself checking the front porch for no reason.

12

Liz and Jackson had tried to talk Sadie out of driving Liz's car.

Determined to help, though, their friend had raced through Indiana's corn and soybean fields, found all the wrong routes in Louisville—"Whaddaya mean this bridge is closed?"—and now, because of interstate construction, was screeching Liz's brand-new tires on winding two-lane roads in Kentucky's forested hills.

To make matters worse, she'd prepared a playlist of country music "to get in the mood" for Nashville.

Liz liked some country songs, but Sadie played only numbers by some guy named Jessy Plank, who sang through his nose, mostly about mean women and bad beer.

Finally, Liz blurted, "This is the worst music I've ever heard."

"Yep. Terrible, isn't it?" Sadie said pleasantly.

Jackson glanced at Liz helplessly as their driver lowered her window and stuck out her head to yell at a passing semi.

After two hours of musical toxic waste and Lavinia, Liz's snooty GPS, chirping directions over the noise, Liz was done. "Sadie, if Jessy Plank's so terrible, why are you playing his songs?"

"Because I feel sorry for him. Nobody's going to buy his music." Driving one-handed down a steep incline, Sadie laid rubber. With the other hand she reached in her purse, pulling out a photo she'd brought along, and handed it to Liz. "Plus, isn't he the cutest thing you ever saw?"

"No!" Jackson yelled from the back seat. "No, he's not! And I'm not spending one more minute listening to him."

"Sheesh. What a grouch." Sadie threw a reproachful look over her shoulder.

"Look out!" Liz screamed.

Afterward, Jackson insisted Sadie had avoided the huge, oncoming pickup truck by driving on two wheels.

"Glad that worked out," their irrepressible friend commented as she continued to zoom along the spiraled road, "but I am a little tired."

Thank God.

When they encountered a barn's driveway, Sadie pulled in. They all got out—mostly to reestablish their sense of gravity.

"Want me to drive?" Jackson, still pale, didn't look like he should.

Liz shook her head. "I know my car better than you do."

He didn't argue.

After riding with Sadie, navigating construction zones seemed easy. When they reached the outskirts of Nashville, Jackson, who had recovered, took the wheel.

They'd decided to stay at a downtown hotel near the location of Innovation Sounds, as they didn't have time to drive all over Nashville. Not cost-effective, but time-effective, Liz tried to tell herself as they pulled into the hotel's parking garage and retrieved their bags.

"Sadie, leave the gun in the trunk." Jackson hadn't used his mayor voice during the trip, but he did now.

"He's right." Liz crossed her arms. "We won't check in until you put it back."

"Oh, all right." Their friend grumbled as she stashed her shotgun. "You forget that everybody in Tennessee has a gun."

"Maybe in their pickups. Not in nice hotels." Jackson slammed the trunk shut.

Fortunately, the hotel clerk, with his friendly drawl, kidded Sadie out of her grumps.

After they'd settled in, a sunset walk around the city raised their spirits, especially as Nashville's famous neon lighting illuminated the streets. They saw the Country Music Hall of Fame and Museum, the Johnny Cash Museum, and other landmarks they might explore at a more leisurely time. A refreshment stop at the Goo Goo Shop, where they watched its legendary chocolatey confections being made by hand, brightened the evening considerably.

"Let's find the Innovation Sounds building tonight," Liz said, "so we won't waste time tomorrow morning."

The street address on the website led them to a complex of tall buildings, old and new, all locked. Like unfriendly giants, they dwarfed the visitors.

"No suite number was listed. I haven't seen any outdoor directories." Liz frowned. "I'd assumed the company was located in a smaller building."

"We'll come here early tomorrow to track it down." Jackson assured her.

"We'll do this, girl." Sadie slapped Liz on the back a little too hard. "If we need to, we'll split up and search."

Her breezy confidence reminded Liz why they had brought Sadie along—driving notwithstanding. Her lame jokes as they walked back to the hotel coaxed smiles to Liz's lips.

Still, she couldn't shake the feeling that somewhere among the sociable Sunday night passersby, watchful eyes followed them.

When they reached the hotel, Sadie retired in her wildly striped robe and weird purple nightcap with a multicolored pom-pom. Her plan for the evening involved making phone calls and munching Goo Goo Clusters while she watched her favorite TV show.

Liz and Jackson took the elevator to a posh rooftop terrace, where they drank in the view of the nighttime city and its many-hued reflections in the Cumberland River. Liz wanted to stay up there all night with Jackson. But tomorrow would require energy and a clear head.

They rode the elevator to the seventh floor, where they unlocked their rooms after a sweet kiss good night. Jackson's proximity soothed thoughts of Liz's earlier uneasiness. And her roommate was sure to scare off any stalker, even without her shotgun.

Suddenly exhausted, Liz changed, set her phone alarm, and dropped into bed. Not even Sadie's snoring would keep her awake tonight.

Early the next morning, Liz, Jackson, and Sadie began their search for the Innovation Sounds offices. Neither Lavinia nor the GPS apps on their phones could give them information on the buildings' layouts. After a frustrating hour of searching together, they split up.

Liz wandered aimlessly through labyrinths of nondescript hallways, constantly looking over her shoulder. Who had trained the architects who had designed these buildings? The CIA?

She often passed dark offices, which seemed strange on a Monday morning. The workers in the inhabited ones wore suits and blank expressions. No one seemed to know anything about Innovation Sounds.

She took refuge in a random courtyard. Its oddly shaped bushes and stark stone benches didn't thrill her aesthetically, but here she could monitor her surroundings better.

Had they wasted time, money, and effort on this trip to try to find a nonexistent company? With the success of "Love, You Are My Friend," surely Innovation Sounds hadn't folded.

Maybe when she rendezvoused with the others, they would have had more luck.

Sure enough, within five minutes, her phone dinged with a text from Sadie. *Found it! See you in a few.*

That's what you think. But with only three wrong turns, Liz navigated to their starting point.

"Man, how did you find them?" Jackson's face was flushed with annoyance. "I kept feeling like I should scatter crumbs so I can find my way back."

Sadie beamed. "When the office people couldn't tell me diddly, I talked to janitors. One really liked my sunflower hat, and we got to talking about crocheting. When I told her why I was here, she said she wasn't supposed to help visitors find places—security rules or something—but she could see I was a nice person, and they didn't have to worry about me."

Liz and Jackson exchanged dubious glances.

"So show us, please." Jackson's patience was shrinking by the minute.

Sadie fairly skipped around the biggest building. They trailed her to two smaller ones behind it. She pointed. "See where those two connect?"

Jackson squinted. "That's weird. They share those floors near the top?"

Liz had visited both buildings—she thought—but hadn't the faintest idea they were joined up there.

"Stick close to me," Sadie said importantly, "because the offices are tucked into the top shared floor. If you don't know it's there, it kind of disappears if you go through the wrong door."

Liz and Jackson shadowed Sadie, meandering through more hallways to elevators in a hidden alcove. When theirs came to a shuddering stop on the fifth floor, Sadie charged forward.

Liz hesitated.

Her friend turned back, gesturing impatiently. "What?"

"I don't know . . ." She turned to Jackson. "It's like we're in some surreal movie. If we leave the elevator, we'll never get back."

"I know exactly what you mean." Jackson sounded too sympathetic. "I felt that way the last time we went shopping at the mall."

She made a face and marched out of the elevator. They hurried down the hall.

Sadie said, "Can you tell we're on the lower shared floor?"

Liz couldn't, and neither could Jackson.

"Not surprised. Had to look out bathroom windows before I figured it out." Sadie gestured to a nondescript door on the right. "That's a stairway and the only access to the upper shared floor."

"Do you get the feeling they don't want to be found?" Now that Liz had pushed past her fears, she took the steps two at a time.

At the top, she threw open the door. Instead of the dark, cave-like corridor she had expected, a small, plant-dotted lobby full of natural light met her gaze.

Liz breathed a prayer as she strode toward the glass entry. Then she halted. "No sign. Are you sure this is the right place?"

"Leona—that's the janitor—brought me here herself. Said they moved in not too long ago."

Liz opened the door and approached a twentysomething Southern belle, who drawled, "May I help you?"

Liz matched her smile, introducing herself and the others. "I probably talked with you the past week about the song, 'Love, You Are My Friend.'"

The secretary's smile shrank. "Yes, I sent your message through the appropriate channels, but we do have people on vacation."

"I understand. But we've driven all the way from Indiana for answers to important questions. Surely someone in your company can help us."

The girl wove apologies into her sort-of refusal. Besides those absent on vacation, some workers were off-site—

"Is anyone here?"

"Only me right now."

"Is *anyone* coming in today?" Sadie asked testily.

The secretary's eyes fastened on Sadie's hat. "I'm so sorry. I'm just not sure. Maybe Ms. Watson. But she's—"

"Would you please call or text Ms. Watson?" Jackson had stepped in front of Liz, flashing his irresistible smile. "Surely she'll want to chat a moment with Trey Edmond fans who have driven such a long way."

"But she's the boss—"

"I'm a boss too." Another brilliant smile. "I want to hear from my customers, so I imagine Ms. Watson will feel the same way."

Slowly, the mesmerized secretary complied. "She says she'll be in sometime today, but she doesn't know if she'll have time to see you."

Just get Ms. Watson in here. We'll sic Jackson on her. Liz said sweetly, "We'll wait here until Ms. Watson comes."

She and Jackson sat on a trendy, uncomfortable sofa while Sadie fidgeted in the only other chair. Liz asked for Ms. Watson's first name—Eleanor—and researched her online. The woman's name appeared in several kinds of social media, though with little personal information. Her business facts were consistent with those of Innovation Sounds' website. She published music and marketed musicians, including several other up-and-coming singers like Trey.

Fortunately, Sadie had brought a Zane Grey Western that would keep her from chattering like a parakeet.

The quiet office would have lulled Liz to sleep, except for the backache generated by the sofa.

The secretary brought a salad to her desk.

"You stay open during the lunch hour?" Sofa torture notwithstanding, Liz hoped so. If they were forced to abandon their vigil, the elusive Ms. Watson might slip in, then out—forever.

The girl nodded. "Aren't y'all hungry? I doubt Ms. Watson will come during the noon hour. We have wonderful restaurants downtown. You'll find some of the best cooking you ever tasted."

Liz's stomach emitted a loud growl. *Forget it,* she chided her rebellious appetite. *No way will she get rid of us.*

Sadie offered, "Want me to go bring something back for us?"

Sending Sadie for takeout always involved risks. But Liz couldn't picture taking a step outside that office door until she'd talked with Ms. Watson, and Jackson couldn't go—his smile power already had proved invaluable.

Besides, Sadie had begun to twitch and pace and talk about motorcycles. She needed a change of scenery. So Liz gave her a grateful smile. "That would be awesome. You know I'm not picky. But remember—no asparagus."

Not long ago, her friend's asparagus obsession had encompassed even desserts.

"I'll remember." Sadie turned to Jackson. "What would you like?"

"I don't know. Surprise me."

"Okay." Sadie zipped out the door.

Jackson looked at Liz. "Maybe I should have rephrased that."

"You think?"

But Sadie returned with the best barbecue pork sandwiches Liz had ever tasted. Steaming, deep-fried okra and mushrooms accompanied them. A satisfactory lunch, though the sweet tea had the taste and consistency of syrup.

After lunch and a short walk in the lobby—Liz would spot Watson if she approached—she felt ready for the encounter.

Unfortunately, Ms. Watson did not come within the next hour. Or the next.

"Maybe she had a change in plans." The sweet dragon guarding Innovation Sounds' portals fluttered long eyelashes.

The secretary disappeared into the back room occasionally, during which times the three perked up their ears. As the afternoon wore on, Liz shamelessly put her ear to the closed door.

Around three o'clock, she thought she heard a different female voice behind the door. "That has to be Watson," she hissed at Jackson and Sadie. "But how did she get in without us seeing her?"

"Trapdoor?" Sadie suggested.

"She's probably been here the whole time," Jackson said, more reasonably.

Liz waved for silence, but she heard only a word or two of their conversation. Unladylike words. What now? Liz hurried to the others. Quickly, they formulated a plan.

When Sweet Dragon returned, Liz fixed her eyes on a novel, and Sadie followed suit. Jackson, however, leaned over the woman's desk, charm oozing from his every cell.

"I realize Ms. Watson is very busy. But isn't there some way we can connect with her before closing?"

The Dragon shrugged. "I'm *so* sorry, sir, but that's just not going to work out."

"What a shame," he said, matching her sweet tone. "We may have to come back tomorrow."

Not what they had planned, but the ploy, whether true or not, produced its desired effect—a look of alarm crossed the heart-shaped face.

Jackson soothed her with an inquiry about local attractions, since they would be spending another night in Nashville. The Dragon should have been a tour guide. In her enthusiasm, she didn't seem to realize he'd worked his way around her desk—or she didn't mind.

When Liz stood and asked the location of the ladies' room, Sweet Dragon barely shifted her gaze from Jackson's face. Liz walked toward the office entrance, then slipped behind the secretary and through the forbidden door.

Liz shot through the empty open office to a closed door in the rear, the indignant Dragon far behind, thanks to stiletto heels. Pasting a smile on her face, Liz barged through the door. "Ms. Watson! So nice to meet you at last."

A black-haired woman sitting at a large desk eyed Liz as if she were a piece of lint on her sleek suit. "How did you get in here?"

How did you *get in here?* Liz widened her smile as Jackson's hand squeezed her shoulder and Sadie stepped up on Liz's other side. The woman's glance locked on Sadie's hat. "Who are you? Are you all insane?"

Liz said, "So sorry to disturb you, Ms. Watson, especially right before closing. You're CEO of this company, correct?"

"Yes." Her tone added that it was none of their business.

"What I want shouldn't take long. I'd like to see the legal documentation that Trey Edmond wrote 'Love, You Are My Friend.' And that you're entitled to a percentage of profits he's made on the song and its recordings."

"And why should I do that?" Ms. Watson aimed a sharp glare at Liz and company, then at the hapless Dragon, wringing her hands at the side. "Stephanie, call security."

"Why not call the police?" Liz leaned over the desk. She pulled out her phone. "Here, I'll call them for you."

The woman's eyes widened, then narrowed. "If I were less tolerant, I would. However, I will comply with your unreasonable demand. Then I expect you to leave immediately." She stood, towering over Liz. Even over Jackson. "Stephanie, print out the documents for that song. Highlight the relevant lines."

Keep smiling. Liz didn't move an inch. She didn't take her eyes from the tight, lovely face. Behind her, the others didn't budge.

When Stephanie returned, Ms. Watson grabbed the sheets of paper and nearly shoved them in Liz's face. "Look. There. And there. Trey Edmond, by the way, is his stage name. His real name is Chad Anderson."

Liz scanned them quickly with her lawyer's eye. Chad Anderson/Trey Edmond had signed the contract, also signed by Eleanor Watson. He affirmed the song was his creation and his property. He'd signed over a percentage of profits to Innovation Sounds in exchange for their publishing and promoting his song.

All in order. And indisputable without the diary. Liz's heart sank. "May I keep this?"

"No, you may not." Ms. Watson snatched the copy.

"By the way, is Trey around? Or have you talked to him lately?" Liz wished they had thought to have Jackson coax that information from Stephanie. "He hasn't been active on his social media for a few days."

One classically shaped eyebrow rose, but Ms. Watson sneered, "I do not play nursemaid to artists. If he neglects promotion, our marketing department deals with that. Now, leave." Her triumphant smile, with its too-white gleam, raked Liz worse than her scowl. "Before I change my mind and call the authorities anyway."

13

At the pizza place they chose for supper, Liz ate one slice, but only nibbled on the second one.

Though Sadie's optimism could annoy Liz like computer pop-ups, her friend helped color the glum evening with her lamest jokes and a perfect imitation of Eleanor Watson.

"Are you all insane?" Sunflowers wiggling, Sadie swept an arm to include the bewildered server and patrons ogling from a neighboring table. "If I were less tolerant, I'd banish you all to the Dungeon of Doom!"

Maybe the day's stress had loosened her own restraints. Liz giggled while Jackson slipped the wary waiter cash and soothed nearby diners somewhat with a murmured, "Please forgive my aunt. They don't have her medication right yet."

Nevertheless, they soon had that corner of the restaurant to themselves.

"Nice and quiet," Sadie licked her fingers with satisfaction. "Just like we wanted."

They hadn't planned to stay another night in Nashville. However, Liz and Jackson joined in a silent sigh of relief when Sadie nixed driving through the night too.

Instead of dwelling on their difficult day as they finished, they shared bits of hometown news Mary Ann and Naomi had texted, including the fact that the Material Girls had made great progress on Liz and Jackson's quilt.

As they talked, Liz's knotted muscles relaxed, but homesickness trickled through her. A return to Pleasant Creek wouldn't ease her complicated life—especially when the chief found out about their Nashville trip—but she missed her inn and her small town. She worried about Steve.

They rose to leave. When Jackson asked about plans for the rest of the evening, Liz said she'd explored enough for today and needed quiet time to think things through. He agreed.

"You're kidding, aren't you?" Sadie stared as if they were aliens. "We're in Music City and you two want to hibernate? How old are you, anyway?"

She consulted an events page and dragged them to a brightly lit storefront pulsing with fiddles, guitars, and lines of dancers. Before Liz knew it, they were doing the "Cowboy Hustle," laughing as if trouble couldn't touch them.

Sadie connected with a group of seniors who must have learned to dance when they learned to walk. They wowed the whole club as spectators clapped, yelled, and whistled.

Liz applauded Sadie, but she couldn't take her eyes from Jackson. The lines in his face had eased, his eyes sparkled, and Liz knew she was marrying the finest man on earth. The chief's words that she'd tried to un-memorize floated through her mind: "It's a special time for you and Jackson. He'd like things to stay nice and uncomplicated for a change, wouldn't he?"

She'd already entangled him in this current mess. But for one night, they could forget their worries. Liz slipped a hand into Jackson's and squeezed. He whirled her onto the dance floor, and they two-stepped along with other couples, oblivious to line dancers in the middle.

They didn't last as long as Sadie, however, who was just warming up.

Jackson whispered, "It's been fun, but I wouldn't mind some quiet time with you."

"Works for me." She touched his cheek.

They said goodbye to Sadie, whose new friends promised to see her safely back to the hotel.

"Don't you worry about her, honey. We always walk in a group," explained Betty Ann, a bright-eyed woman probably in her seventies. "And Charlie and Mel over there are retired Marine officers."

Reassured, Liz and Jackson took a leisurely walk back to the hotel and once again found their favorite vistas on the sparsely populated rooftop terrace.

Tonight, the city glowed like a treasure chest of jewels scattered on dark velvet.

"Sometimes I forget you're such an awesome dancer," Liz told him.

"Only when I'm dancing with you." He spun her into his arms with a chuckle, then sobered. "I wish the rest of the trip could have been as relaxing for you."

"For me?" Liz shook her head. "Once again, I've dragged you into situations no one should have to deal with. I'm complicated with a capital C."

"I wouldn't mind a few more dates without needing bodyguards," Jackson admitted, his eyes twinkling. "But I've never met anyone like you, Liz. Your 'complications' and how you handle them—with intelligence and courage and caring—it's part of what I love about you."

"I hope you feel that way in twenty years," she teased.

"I will if I'm still alive."

Their laughter loosened the tautness of the evening's underlying tension: What action should they take next?

"Not sure there's anything else we can do here," Jackson said, as if reading her mind. "At this point, Ms. Watson will yell, 'Harassment!' if we go near her building."

"True. If only we'd uncovered something." Liz pushed back an annoying strand of hair. "Just a shred of evidence that might help unravel what's going on. A hint of where to look for Geoffrey . . . Trey . . . Chad. Whatever his name is." She made a face.

"I think we shook the trees a little. At least, you did. What were you thinking, offering to call the police on us?"

"I wanted to see how Watson would react. It's called a bluff." Liz paused, reliving the scene. "She really didn't want the police involved—though I'd have called them if someone came charging into my office and demanded to see private legal documents. She was right. My demand *was* unreasonable. Why did she give in?"

"If she simply wanted to get rid of us, she could have trumped us with the police card. Or security," Jackson agreed.

"Instead, Watson wanted to convince us that we had no case. That would make us stop asking questions. However, she also reacted for a split second when I asked about Trey, though she covered pretty well."

"I don't think we'll know how successful we were until we see a few ripples from the visit. So relax tonight, will you?"

"If I can get her face out of my head." Liz scrunched her eyes. "She looked like a villainess from a cartoon movie—beautiful and evil."

"Evil, certainly. But not as beautiful as you."

Great answer.

Jackson bought them drinks, and they claimed ownership of one of the "conversation areas" in a corner of the terrace. Sitting under the stars, the fragrance from pots of roses perfuming the air, they talked about their wedding. Blissful—until the subject of their song arose.

The conversation wandered back to Eleanor Watson. "She does have the law on her side," Liz admitted, "unless I recover the diary or find some other evidence that Trey didn't write that song."

"Did your mother ever mention your dad's writing it?"

"No. I think it was something special between them—and Mom

tended to keep her feelings private. She may have sung it when she missed him the most." Her eyes moistened.

"Did they write letters? You might find the lyrics in one of them."

"Mom didn't leave any among her papers. Not surprising, since they met and married in Boston and lived there together until my father died. There wouldn't have been any need for letters." She gave a deep sigh and toyed with her glass. "I want so much for Kiera to sing Dad's song at our wedding. But with all that's happening—"

"She will sing it, regardless of Geoffrey or Watson or anyone else." Jackson's firm words sent a sweet thrill through her. "No one can take that away from us."

Later, when they again split up at their respective rooms, the fun music of the evening echoed through Liz's head, and once again, she danced with Jackson in her mind, loving his moves, loving him. When she chided herself about the late hour, the words of their wedding song lilted through her mind and sang her to sleep.

An impossibly loud ringing nearly sent Liz to the hotel room ceiling. Had her roommate set her alarm at the same volume level as her music? "Turn it off, Sadie!"

"Turn what off?" Sadie sat up, the colorful pom-pom on her nightcap quivering with indignation. "I didn't turn anything on!"

Someone pounded on their door. "Liz! Sadie! Fire!"

Jackson. Liz's grogginess fled. She threw on a robe, unlocked the door, and yanked it open.

"Hurry!" Jackson, clad in pajama pants and a T-shirt, grabbed her hand. "Come on, Sadie! Get to the stairs!"

Other hotel guests clad in nightdress sprinted down the hall. Jackson, Liz, and Sadie banged on any closed doors they encountered. "Fire!"

They had descended several flights of steps before Liz realized she hadn't seen or smelled smoke. The fire must be burning on the opposite side of the hotel.

They burst through the exit onto the sidewalk. Police were pulling up in squad cars and shouting for guests and employees to move away. Wailing fire trucks, their lights and sirens slicing through the darkness, halted in front of the hotel. Firefighters in rubber boots and coats leaped from trucks and ran for the hotel. Ambulances added their shrieks to the cacophony.

Liz, Jackson, and Sadie jogged down the block until they could hear each other's voices.

Many onlookers wore nightclothes. But Sadie's iridescent robe of many colors and her pom-pom nightcap practically glowed in the dark. At least they wouldn't lose her in the crowd of awakened downtown dwellers and other tourists. Many stopped dead in their tracks when they saw Sadie.

She modeled her robe as if on a runway. "Perfect evening attire, don't you think?" she said with a snobby accent.

Most hurried on, though Liz heard one child ask, "Mommy, was that an alien?"

Liz turned her attention back to the hotel. She still didn't see fire or smoke. "Maybe it was a false alarm?"

Jackson watched police cars blocking a nearby intersection. "I might get a straight story from them."

She and Sadie watched him jog up to an officer.

"He's used to knowing what's going on," Sadie remarked, "but this ain't Pleasant Creek."

It certainly wasn't. The ruckus seemed to increase, rather than resolve. Not far away. Liz watched a video crew filming a TV reporter's interview with a tall man wearing a denim jacket. He looked vaguely familiar.

Liz tugged on Sadie's sleeve. "Bet we'll learn something there."

They joined the large number of listeners.

The reporter asked, "When did you first hear about the bomb threat, Lake?"

Bomb threat? Liz and Sadie exchanged stares.

"Not real sure, but when that fire alarm woke me up, the clock said a little after three."

"That's Lake Carson," Sadie breathed. "He won all those CMA awards last year. He must have performed here this past weekend."

The singer continued, "My agent ran me down the stairs and outside. He talked to the hotel people, and they said the guy on the phone was ranting about something and not making a lot of sense." Lake shook his head. "Probably had a few too many."

He steered the interviewer toward his upcoming performances, and Liz lost interest, especially when she saw people reentering the hotel. Apparently, the authorities had sounded an all clear. But where was Jackson?

Surely if he couldn't see Liz, he could spot Sadie.

Then she saw him, jogging toward her, neon lights and streetlights shining on his hair.

In these frightening hours, the sight of him lifted her heart.

Crack! Crack! Crack!

Why was someone celebrating this night with fireworks?

"Get down, Liz!" Jackson hurtled through the air and crushed her into the sidewalk as screams erupted around them. He reached out and yanked Sadie down beside them.

Not firecrackers. Not a celebration.

Gunshots.

14

"Roll under the van!" Jackson shoved Liz and Sadie toward the nearest vehicle as several more shots were fired. Liz scrambled under the blue van as people all around took cover. Peering out, Liz saw uniformed legs running, presumably in the direction of the shooter.

A twangy accent spoke in the darkness. "Somebody is nuts out there."

Sadie turned her phone into a flashlight. Her voice lowered to tones of reverence. "Lake Carson!"

"The same. 'Cool country,' that's me." His wide stage smile practically glowed in the dark.

Cowering under a van, fearing for their lives, this guy was promoting himself? Liz guessed that for a performer, it came as naturally as breathing.

Jackson said, "If the shooter is still loose, we don't want to give him a target. It's quieter out there now, so let's keep our voices down. You need to dim that, Sadie."

She turned off her flashlight.

The figure next to Lake said in a low voice, "I'm Elle Rizer, Channel 17 News." The reporter who had been interviewing Lake earlier now fidgeted beside him in the shadows.

Though they couldn't see her clearly, Liz, Jackson, and Sadie introduced themselves.

"I hope y'all don't think too badly of Nashville," Elle said. "Haven't spent many Tuesday evenings downtown hiding under a van." She fiddled with something. "I think my pocket recorder works." A click. "Yes! Lake, let's get past the bomb scare and talk about the alleged shooting."

Lake shifted, then spoke in the same guarded voice. "Yeah, I thought some truck was backfirin' until people started hittin' the ground, and you and me ended up here."

"I wasn't sure we were going to make it." The reporter's voice trembled. She reined in her shakiness, though, continuing to interview him.

And I thought this morning was surreal. Liz once had been bound and gagged and stuffed into a van. But she'd never spent time under one with a country singing star and a reporter while bullets whizzed through the air outside.

Jackson nudged her. "Weren't we saying something earlier about complications?"

"This is why you love me, right?" she whispered. She wriggled sideways, hoping to get a better view of the street.

Almost empty, as it should be at past three in the morning. Was everyone still cowering in hiding places? She and Jackson again spotted pairs of uniformed legs on the other side of the street, presumably belonging to police. But their knees were slightly bent, as if in a defensive position.

Elle was pressing Lake. "If this incident does involve a shooter, do you have any idea why here, why now? Do you think he might have been aiming for you?"

He gave an audible gulp in the darkness. Lake said slowly, "Well, you always make enemies in this business."

He'd lost his bravado, so Elle held her microphone toward Sadie. "Could you tell me what you saw when the alleged shots were fired?"

Sadie snorted. "Nothing alleged about it. Somebody was shooting from across the street—probably from one of those empty buildings."

"You seem pretty sure, Ms.—"

"Sadie Schwarzentruber. S-c-h-w-a-r-z-e-n-t-r-u-b-e-r. Spell it right, please. From Pleasant Creek, Indiana. I've been around guns all my life, and I could tell from the sound."

Liz tensed. How much would Sadie say? Surely, she wouldn't reveal their reason for their Nashville trip!

Jackson, his thoughts apparently following similar paths, grasped Liz's wrist as if warning her. But who could silence Sadie?

Predictably, Elle zeroed in on their qualms. "That's quite a haul. What are you doing in Nashville?"

"I'm going to audition for the Senior Singing Showdown television competition," Sadie said. "We're in town to get some inspiration."

Liz flopped back on the hard asphalt, trying not to laugh. Would an audio of Sadie's interview air on Nashville's morning news? Liz felt Jackson's ribs shake with suppressed laughter.

Suddenly, feet and a weathered face appeared at the van's edge, along with a blinding flashlight. "Y'all having a picnic under here?"

A policeman.

"No, sir." Jackson switched to his mayor's voice. "We hid when the shots were fired."

"Well, you can come out now. We've searched the immediate area thoroughly. Looks like the shooter's fled the scene."

Liz couldn't crawl out from under the van fast enough. Her spurt of energy died, though, as she tried to stretch her cramped muscles. Oh, for a nice hot bath!

"You're Lake Carson, aren't you?"

At the policeman's query, the singing star donned his stage smile again. "Sure am. 'Cool country,' that's—"

"You were doing a TV interview when the shooting started."

"Yes, with me." Elle introduced herself.

"I know you're probably tired out, but we need to talk to you." The friendly officer, who told them he was Patrolman Matthews, made a quick call. A burly plainclothes guy materialized who introduced himself as Detective Hawkins.

Liz had to know. "Was anyone hurt?"

"No, everybody's like you. Tired, but doing fine."

"Tired" was right. Her legs, limp as rubber bands, didn't want to hold up the rest of her. For the first time, her brain shifted from survival mode to a "why?" phase. Why the shooting? Why the bomb scare? With the juxtaposition of the two, surely they were connected.

For the next hour, Liz and the others answered questions, positioned, and repositioned themselves in spots where they had stood during the shooting while officers measured and recorded.

At the sight of bullet holes in the wall behind the interview spot, Liz's stomach lurched again. Three shots had struck perilously close to her and Sadie. Three more had hit near Lake.

From what Liz could gather during the interviews, the shooter had targeted their area exclusively. When she, Jackson, and Sadie were released, the detective had continued to talk with a reluctant Lake, Elle hovering nearby.

"Can we stay a minute longer?" Liz whispered to Jackson and Sadie.

He nodded reluctantly. "Okay. But what excuse can we give for hanging around?"

"I'll pretend I'm pooped," said Sadie. "Though that's not a hard sell." Sadie could play her old-lady card well when she chose to. She whined to an officer, "I can't walk back all that way! I need to sit down."

He allowed her to sit in his patrol car.

Jackson explained that they would wait and escort Sadie back to the hotel when she felt better.

Meanwhile, Liz's ears caught conversation snippets here and there. Hawkins didn't buy the singer's "In this business, you always make enemies." After promising Elle an exclusive interview later—thus ridding himself of her recorder, phone, and inquisitive questions—Detective Hawkins asked Lake for specifics about acquaintances who might hold grudges against him.

As he answered, the singer fiddled with the cowboy hat he'd recovered from the sidewalk. He explained that some competitors were jealous of his talent. They couldn't stand Lake's ability to sell out concerts. "Plus, um, well, I owe a lot of money for . . . personal reasons."

Liz could imagine the nature of his "personal reasons." If Lake had overextended himself by glitzy living, gambling, or drugs—or some combination thereof—loan sharks or other vengeful creditors might want to get rid of him.

It made sense. Famous guy, bad past or present, and revenge attempt. Since Lake was perpetually surrounded by people—hadn't Lake's agent dragged him outside during the bomb threat?—a killer would have to maneuver him into a vulnerable position—one in which the assassin could kill from afar and escape quickly.

At the word "assassin," Eleanor Watson's narrow-eyed face popped into Liz's mind.

What is with you? Her imagination was trying to turn the woman into a boogeyman. Liz shook the image from her head.

But she failed to rid herself of one cold, clear thought: The aforementioned strategy of bomb threat/shooting would also work if Watson wanted to get rid of *them*.

Liz's lungs flattened.

Breathe. Breathe. Get oxygen to the brain so such bizarre ideas stop popping up.

Yes, something strange was going on with her father's song, Geoffrey, and Innovation Sounds.

But a bomb threat and ambush attempt, possibly by an assassin in a designer suit?

Liz shook her head. She needed sleep. Lots of it.

She steered her attention back to Lake. He hadn't yet mentioned the women in his past, but given his good looks and fame, he probably possessed a few fans-turned-foes. Maybe one had gone off the deep end.

Hawkins began to explore those possibilities, but before he probed too deeply, he threw a glance toward Matthews. It was a Stan Houghton look Liz knew well: *Get rid of any superfluous ears in the vicinity.*

The officer accosted Sadie, but his gaze took in Liz and Jackson. "You feeling better, ma'am?"

Sadie thanked him. "Yes, I think I can walk now."

Matthews continued, "Since y'all are from out of state, Detective Hawkins asked if you could stop in at the downtown police station for a few minutes before you leave Nashville, just to confirm things."

They nodded. Liz scanned the street again.

She sensed the officer's gaze. "You're safe, ma'am. Shooter's nowhere around. Have a good rest." He touched his hat and walked back to Hawkins and Lake.

Liz and company headed down the street, beginning to stir with the lightening of the black sky.

Jackson rubbed his neck. "I wouldn't mind a few more hours of sleep before driving back."

"I wouldn't mind sleeping until noon," Sadie informed him.

Before retiring, though, wafting fragrances from a nearby bakery called them into breakfast.

Liz brushed the street's grime from her robe. "Do we dare go in looking like this?" She couldn't help giving Sadie's getup a pointed look.

Her friend shrugged. "Who cares? I say we should celebrate being alive."

"I'm with you." Jackson opened the door. Its bell jangled like

Sweet Everything's. They ate cinnamon rolls that were delicious, but not incredible like Naomi's.

The ripple of Liz's homesickness grew into a wave of anticipation. Tonight she'd sleep in her own bed in her own inn. She'd see Steve. Though Caitlyn had reported nothing but progress, the mom in Liz had to see for herself.

After such a rough night, she was considering a second cinnamon roll when her phone rang.

"It's the chief." *Great.* Would he interrogate her about this trip?

"He's probably found Geoffrey," Jackson encouraged.

"Liz, can you come home?" Stan's odd tone sounded an alarm louder than the bomb scare's. "We found Geoffrey out near River Road last night. He's been dead several days."

15

Liz's hand, holding the phone, sank to her lap.

"What's wrong?"

Sadie grabbed the phone. "What's happening, Chief?"

Her squawked "What?" registered in Liz's hearing, but the rest of Sadie's side of the conversation faded into the pleasant music playing in the background.

From the look on Jackson's face, he'd already deduced that Geoffrey was dead, but Liz told him anyway. Sparks seemed to fly from the very words, sparks that fed the flash fire inside. "Why didn't he tell me what was going on? Maybe I could have helped him. But no, he kept lying. He wouldn't tell me the truth."

Jackson said nothing, but simply held her while Sadie finished the phone call. For once, she remained silent too, her hand warm on Liz's shoulder.

Finally, Liz raised her head. Sympathetic glances met hers from other customers and bakery employees, for which she was grateful. Nevertheless, they couldn't talk where they were. "Let's go."

One of the bakery's employees brought her a steaming cup of coffee to go. "Don't know what your trouble is, darlin', but I hope this will help get you through the day."

The woman's kindness bloomed amid the past twenty-four hours like a marigold in a dump. "Thank you."

They hung a *Do Not Disturb* sign on Liz and Sadie's room, and then gathered around a small table near the window, where Liz didn't feel as if the walls were closing in.

The speed-walk with the others to the hotel had helped clear her head. Maybe now she could make sense. "Did—did the chief give any details about Geoffrey?"

"Not many," Sadie shook her head. "He hadn't received the autopsy report. He did say, though, that he thought Geoffrey had been poisoned."

"Poisoned?" The hair on Liz's neck rose. "When he spoke to me, the chief said Geoffrey had died several days ago. Eleanor Watson was here in Nashville yesterday, but that doesn't mean she was here at the time of his death."

"A strong possibility." Jackson clasped his hands behind his head. "Yet why would Watson do that? Geoffrey was successful, with the possibility of becoming a superstar."

"You don't kill the goose that lays the golden eggs," Sadie chimed in.

"Unless, for some reason, Geoffrey had turned against her." Liz took another gulp of coffee. "Maybe Innovation Sounds had invested heavily in him and 'Love, You Are My Friend,' and then she'd found out he didn't really write it. But you generally fire people for doing things like that or sue them. Besides, if Geoffrey was the burglar who took my diary—and my proof that he didn't write the song—why would Watson kill him?"

She thought she'd gotten a grip, but her voice trembled.

Jackson took her hand. "I know you really hoped he was your dad's brother."

"More than I realized." She gripped her head. "I still don't know that he *wasn't* my uncle. I would have shared royalties with him. All he had to do was tell the truth."

Sadie patted Liz's shoulder, but her eyes blazed. "If he was, this was an awful mess to dump on you right before your wedding." Her voice softened. "I know Geoffrey's death is hard on you, hon, but we gotta think about this bomb threat and shooting thing some more."

"I know." Liz straightened. "We don't know why Watson might eliminate him. But if she did, she wouldn't hesitate to take out anyone else who gets in her way. Like us."

"That detective acted like he already had the whole thing figured out." Sadie imitated Detective Hawkins's gruff voice: "'The shooter almost hit Lake three times and missed him wider three times.'" She lapsed into her regular voice again. "The shots that just missed us."

Liz nodded. "He assumed Lake was the target because he's a celebrity. A celebrity with a history and maybe some habits that have gotten him into trouble. It's a reasonable assumption."

"But reasonable isn't always right," Sadie said. "What if—"

"What if, instead, Watson—or some creep she hired—was aiming for Liz?" Jackson's eyes went cold, and Liz shivered involuntarily. Jackson jumped up. "We don't know what weapons or observation tools this shooter has access to"—he yanked the curtains shut—"but we'd better not wait until we find out." He helped the others shift the table away from the window.

When they'd resettled, Sadie lamented, "We don't have a bit of proof."

"I'm not going to march into Watson's office again and accuse her." Liz tried to shove that picture from her mind. "But didn't that officer ask us to stop by the station before we left? Can't we tell him what we know and ask him to consider our viewpoint when they're looking at ballistics and so on?"

Jackson frowned. "Maybe if we don't name any names. We don't want to accuse Watson if she's innocent."

"True," Liz agreed, "though 'innocent' and Watson seem an oxymoron." Her head felt too heavy to hold up. She leaned her chin on her hand. "Perhaps if we tell the police about Geoffrey's connection to the music industry here, the burglaries, and now his murder . . ." She still couldn't believe he was dead.

"We could give them Stan's contact information to confirm our stories," Jackson suggested.

"The chief may not appreciate that," she warned. "But if anyone could get away with it, it would be you."

Sadie said, "I hope we can talk with that nice patrolman who let me sit in his car. I'll bet he'd be more open-minded than the detective."

"You're probably right. But before we talk with anyone, let's rest." Jackson peered at Liz. "You have to promise that you'll let go of all of this and sleep."

Right now, that presented the easiest promise she'd ever made. Liz's eyes closed almost before she reached the bed. Through a fog she heard Jackson leave and Sadie trying the deadbolt.

And that was all.

Much later that morning, after checking out, they approached the modern, many-windowed building that housed Nashville's downtown precinct. Thankfully, Liz had lost the sense they were being followed.

At the front desk, Jackson asked to see Officer Matthews. He came out to the front desk in a short time and then obligingly took them back to his cubicle.

When they explained their theory, the patrolman stared as if they were newly arrived from Neptune. "You think those bullets were meant for you?"

"Quite possibly for Liz." Jackson leaned forward.

Seeing Jackson had garnered Matthews's ear, Liz let him explain their rationale. Her fiancé deftly generalized their suspicion of "someone in the music industry" possibly connected with the death of Geoffrey Teal without naming who that someone might be. When Jackson offered the officer Stan's number and e-mail, Matthews readily accepted it, true interest sparking in his eyes.

"We understand that you don't have time to chase after every theory the public throws at you," Jackson said. "But I think you'll find that we have adequate reasons for concern."

Amazingly, Sadie kept her mouth shut. Almost.

"You really ought to listen to the mayor." She shook a finger at Matthews. "You should talk to Liz too. Why, she's probably solved as many murders as you have."

Fortunately, he seemed to be an expert in dealing with vehement old ladies. But did he consider Jackson and Liz equally imaginative?

Jackson seemed optimistic as they left the station. "Matthews is the kind of guy who will follow through."

They'd done what they could do. Now, despite having to face Geoffrey's death, Liz's inner GPS locked on *home*. Even though it was near lunchtime, she proposed, "Let's drive a couple of hours, then stop to eat."

"No way." Jackson dug in his heels. "One cinnamon roll at the crack of dawn won't do me for 'a couple of hours.' I'm not going anywhere but a restaurant."

They found one, and Liz had to admit the sumptuous Southern lunch they enjoyed compensated for her backing down. "The sausage gravy and biscuits are truly amazing. And who knew grits could taste so good?"

"You've never tasted them until you've eaten them in the South." Jackson savored another mouthful of cheddar grits mixed with his over-easy eggs.

Afterward, he took the wheel first. Given their earlier adventures, they'd planned an alternate route that included more scenic landscapes and fewer bulldozers. With every mile, Liz gratefully absorbed the tranquility as Jackson, then she drove through Tennessee and Kentucky. They'd gently edged Sadie to do the final leg in Indiana, hoping familiar territory and flatter land would preserve their lives and sanity. Finally, they made the turnoff to Pleasant Creek without incident.

Approaching the Olde Mansion Inn, Liz drank in its lovely Victorian lines and its gingerbread trim, white and lacy against its brick-red sides as if freshly starched. The friendly front porch seemed to throw open its arms, and when Sadie parked the car, Liz ignored the rough stop and ran up the steps of her inn.

She'd been gone only two days, yet it seemed like months. She didn't mind nearly tripping over Beans, who opened an eye in his equivalent of an ecstatic greeting. Mary Ann, who had stayed late at Sew Welcome, met Liz in the rotunda with her usual motherly hug. She hugged Jackson and Sadie too, who was cooing over Beans, positive he had suffered greatly in her absence.

But something in Mary Ann's manner seemed off, as if Liz had tasted her golden, perfect pie and found it—gasp!—underbaked.

Her musings were interrupted by Steve, who'd heard the ruckus from Liz's quarters. He pushed a rolling walker into the rotunda, followed by Caitlyn. After hugs and "Are you all rights?" they adjourned to the sitting room, where Steve filled them in on Dr. Sam's latest report.

"My balance is improving, but with this concussion, Doc wants to make sure I don't fall. I hate this thing"—he smacked the walker—"but it helps me move around." He wasn't sure, though, that his having the walker was good for Caitlyn. "She's not waiting on me anymore. She's gonna forget how to be a nurse."

Caitlyn swatted him.

Under the light banter, Liz detected forced cheerfulness, similar to Mary Ann's, in both her son and Caitlyn.

What was that all about? What did they know that she didn't?

She cast an eye at Sadie to see if she'd noticed anything questionable. But Sadie, who'd hauled a drowsy Beans into the sitting room to share the evening, saw little else but him.

Knock it off, Liz. Steve's injuries, Geoffrey's death, and their

Nashville adventures had cultivated an unhealthy crop of paranoia. She was reading deception into the behavior of her beloved son and friends.

Mary Ann did give Liz pause, though, when the legendary pie baker presented two enormous, beautifully golden, apple pies. She cut Liz her usual gargantuan slice and plopped ice cream on top. While the others joined her in dishing out compliments, Liz slid her fork under the crust and lifted it. It was perfectly baked, no pale doughiness concealed there. And there was no pretense in Mary Ann either.

"Something wrong with your pie, dear?" Her friend's sharp eyes had fastened on her.

"Goodness, no." Liz crammed a huge bite into her mouth. Her wholehearted "Mmm!" must have satisfied Mary Ann. She returned to cutting Jackson and Steve second portions, which neither seemed to mind. Dessert loosened everyone's tongues and laughter rang out.

Liz, Jackson, and Sadie had kept everyone abreast of the shooting via phone, but now Sadie reenacted the entire incident.

Naomi, too, seemed unusually reserved when she arrived, but she soon joined in the ribbing. The fun evening matched any the Girls had ever enjoyed.

Watching Steve act like himself refreshed Liz far more than an early bedtime. She let the charm of her dining room, with its polished antique mahogany table and buffet, embroidered linen runner and delicate china, seep through her.

Perhaps someone had shot at her in Nashville, perhaps not, but nothing would prevent her from reveling in the joy of home.

Eventually, though, Steve drooped. Dr. Sam had prescribed a strict diet of no excitement before Liz left. Improvement or not, he still needed to rest. After traveling all day, Liz wouldn't mind it herself. She dropped a hint that Steve looked tired.

No one seemed to hear.

Caitlyn didn't concern herself with subtlety. "Party's over," she announced. "Steve needs sleep. He won't get it if you're all here. Take your noisy selves home."

He shot barbs about running his life, but Caitlyn shrugged them off. "Time for me to go home too. I have to work tomorrow."

With a wave, she headed out the back way, escorted by Steve. Naomi, who also had to rise early, hurried home. Mary Ann and Sadie headed for the parking lot.

"Gotta check on my animals." Sadie jumped into her pink Jeep and roared off.

Liz and Jackson lingered on the porch, watching the old-fashioned streetlights tease the gold- and scarlet-tipped maples and inhaling the gentle briskness of early autumn night breezes.

He finally kissed her and left, and Liz headed for her quarters. No Steve yet.

She'd told him to continue sleeping in her bedroom, as he certainly wouldn't fit on her sofa. Liz debated whether to stay upstairs in a guest room, but despite Caitlyn's assurances, couldn't bring herself to sleep that far away from Steve. What if he needed help during the night? So Liz spread sheets and a light blanket on the sofa.

She wouldn't sleep in her own bed, but Liz still savored the sight of her teakettle, her dishes, her sofa. Had anyone remembered to water her castor bean plant? She glanced toward the window.

There was an empty space. Had the plant died? She'd left it healthy and flourishing, practically taking over the window. How could anyone kill it in only two days?

Steve opened the door and slowly rolled his walker inside. "I'm more bushed than I thought."

"Thank goodness Caitlyn made everyone go home."

"She'd make a great sergeant."

Liz considered waiting until morning to mention the castor bean plant, but curiosity prompted her. "Um, did somebody move my plant?"

Steve turned sharply, then dropped onto the sofa with his head in his hands. "Chief Houghton has it."

"The chief took my plant?" Was the boy hallucinating? Liz pulled out her phone. "Is your head hurting? I'd better call Dr. Sam—"

"I'm not crazy. Stan has it." Steve finally looked up at her. "He got the autopsy report on Teal. He died of ricin poisoning, which is derived from castor beans. Mom, the chief thinks the poison came from your plant."

16

"I wish Steve hadn't dropped that bomb on you last night." Stan had joined Liz in her four-season room in a vain effort to avoid the remodeling racket upstairs.

He continued, "We'd hoped to let you relax after all that Nashville excitement. But I can understand how Steve couldn't hold back. Knowing you, you bullied him into telling you."

Still numb, Liz remained silent. How could Geoffrey's gift have turned into the weapon that killed him? But facts were facts. She'd researched castor bean plants for half the night, discovering that the fibers inside only five beans could kill an adult within days, even hours.

"Sorry I had to borrow your plant."

"I don't want it back." If Liz never saw one again, it would be too soon.

"And I wish I didn't have to bug you, with the wedding coming up."

That odd note in Stan's voice, the same she'd perceived during his Nashville call, was there again. It matched that weirdness she'd noticed in Mary Ann, Steve, and even Naomi last night. Liz stared at the untasted coffee in her favorite mug. "You have to find out who killed him."

He said too quickly, "I'm not pointing a finger at suspects yet. Anybody can own a castor bean plant. Actually, that's where castor oil comes from. No wonder I hated that stuff when I was a kid." He gave a mirthless laugh. "But since Geoffrey stayed here right before he died . . . you understand why I also have to ask if we can inspect your inn."

"Of course." She wished he would yell at her for going to Nashville. Anything but this artificial courtesy.

But he continued in the same contrived tone, eyes fixed on the lake scene behind her. "We found ricin in the remains of a snack in Teal's backpack. After several days, it was hard to tell what it was, especially with critters in the woods. But it looked like cake with little black dots in it."

Poppy seed bread.

She struggled to breathe normally. While Stan sounded as if he were tossing out casual comments, she knew better. He'd remembered that Geoffrey liked hers. But the chief didn't know she'd given the musician a loaf before he checked out.

How had someone tampered with the bread? She told Stan as much as she could remember about the bread.

He eyed her speculatively, then changed the subject. "By the way, Geoffrey Teal wasn't his real name."

She nodded. "Ms. Watson said his stage name was Trey Edmond, but his real name was Chad Anderson."

"Consider it confirmed. His fingerprints told us he has a record. He had two assault charges that resulted in jail time in his twenties. One was for assaulting his tae kwon do instructor. Hurt him pretty bad."

Charming, considerate Geoffrey. Liz closed her eyes. Yes, given that background, he could have bested Steve, especially if he caught him with his guard down.

The chief told her Geoffrey's birth date. Liz consulted the notes on her phone. "That matches what he told me, but if his real name was Anderson, the birth certificate he waved in front of my nose had to be fake."

The chief nodded slowly. "He certainly had a lot of names."

Liz had to admit the chances of Geoffrey's claim to her father's family tree had shrunk to nearly nothing. Liz dropped her head into her hands. In grieving for Geoffrey, she'd almost forgotten the hope that had danced just out of her reach—that a living relative of her father could attend her wedding.

She finally looked up to see the chief blinking rapidly. He must have been thinking something similar.

Within a second, he had dried his eyes and his tone. "I talked to Jackson about Nashville. You think somebody took a shot at you?"

"I don't know what to believe." She rubbed temples that had throbbed all night.

"I spoke with the Nashville police, a detective named Hawkins who's in charge of the case." Stan gave her a searching look. "He seemed sure that singer, Carson, was the target."

"Yeah, Hawkins interviewed us." She almost suggested that he contact Officer Matthews. But why? The patrolman had been nice, nothing more. "Did Jackson tell you about Innovation Sounds?"

"Yeah, I heard about your run-in with Ms. Watson. I wasn't exactly surprised." The chief grimaced. "She was still mad this morning when I contacted her. Said it wasn't enough that her promising musician was dead, but she also had to deal with crazies barging into her office."

Liz could imagine how respectable the CEO could sound when necessary.

Maybe Jackson had explained their rationale, but with no evidence to counter Watson's documentation, she didn't bother to elaborate. Speaking took too much effort just now anyway.

"We've combed the Internet for leads to Teal's—Anderson's—family, but no luck. I asked Ms. Watson if she knew of any, but she didn't. Not even an emergency contact. Didn't seem interested in attending his service either, which kind of surprised me."

It didn't surprise Liz. But the word *service* triggered a fresh, ugly spurt of reality into her day.

She tried to keep her voice even. "When and where will the service be?"

Concern flickered in the chief's face, but he said, "Yoder's, tomorrow at eleven. We thought it best to cremate Teal, in case the family shows up and wants to move his remains."

Liz nodded numbly. Maybe Geoffrey did have a lost mother, as he claimed. Perhaps someday she might get her head on straight and come looking for her son.

"Guess we'd better start the inspection." The chief patted her hand awkwardly, then stood. "We'll finish this ASAP so you can rest after your trip."

Right. Like she'd rested last night. "Whatever you have to do."

Stan's phone rang. He grabbed it as if eager to talk to someone else.

Liz unlocked doors, left her coffee, and headed outside to her bench behind the lilacs. Surely they wouldn't check her bench for evidence, would they?

The sunny morning seemed a mockery. She didn't want to greet the sky, with its happy clouds chasing each other like lambs. So she closed her eyes and simply breathed a while.

Liz felt rather than heard Stan's approach behind her. For a stocky guy, he could move like a cat.

"Well?" Liz asked.

The chief's eyes fixed over her shoulder at the flowerless bushes. He said in a flat tone, "I'm done in there. I'll let you know in a day or two."

Bright-blue patch to flowered patch to cream-colored patch to light-blue patch—because of Opal's and Sadie's flawless cutting, the edges of the quilt pieces fit together perfectly.

Unlike the pieces of her life. Liz's fingers trembled as she basted.

Stan had phoned, saying he'd receive test results by tomorrow morning. Could she meet with him then? After hanging up, she'd burst into Sew Welcome and blurted her fears.

Mary Ann went into command mode. "Call the Girls and we'll work on your quilt tonight. I'll see if Miriam and your aunt Ruth can come too."

Liz had protested fruitlessly, not wanting to explain again, answer more questions, maintain a stiff smile. Nor did she want to lose her composure, as she almost did when Miriam and Aunt Ruth engulfed her in loving embraces.

The others made up the usual chitchat and banter, and Liz even summoned a few natural smiles.

Still, comfortable silences occasionally compressed into vacuums. Liz couldn't lose the shadow that followed her every move. Even the sparkle of Jackson's diamond on her finger dimmed.

"I know what *you* need." Sadie poked Liz with an elbow. "You need a song. C'mon, Opal. Let's sing Liz a duet."

Before Liz could respond, Sadie dragged Opal away from her cutting table. "Let's sing 'You Can't Roller-Skate in a Buffalo Herd.'"

Liz gaped at her friend.

"You don't know that song?" Sadie didn't let Liz's ignorance bother her. Opal didn't either. She whined a high, thin harmony to Sadie's bellowing lyrics about roller skating and buffalo, showering in parakeet cages, and other ridiculous concepts, but choosing to be happy anyway.

Liz covered her ears. "That's not a real song, is it?" she demanded.

"Actually, it's one of my favorites." Mary Ann, waving her scissors, joined in while Naomi and Caitlyn clung to each other, giggling.

Liz thought the "song" couldn't get worse until familiar, awful wobbles joined in. Yodeling! Miriam and Aunt Ruth, eyes dancing with mischief under their Kapps, knew perfectly well that Liz despised the Amish musical pastime.

At the height of the discordant cacophony, Jackson walked in. He froze.

At the look of puzzled horror on his face, Liz collapsed in a fit of giggles, and the rest of the group followed suit.

A big smile broke through on his incredulous face. "Is—is this some secret woman therapy?"

"The best." Liz wiped her eyes. "They just sang me a song even worse than Jessy Plank's. I feel lots better."

"I don't get it, but anything goes if it makes you laugh."

"Now she's going to model her wedding dress, so you have to leave." Mary Ann pointed imperiously toward the door.

"You're kicking me out already?"

"Yes, but take a cinnamon roll with you." Naomi wrapped one in a napkin for him.

Jackson winked at Liz before Sadie and Caitlyn shoved him out Sew Welcome's door and locked it. Through the glass, he pantomimed that he would call her later.

Mary Ann glared at him sternly until he comically hung his head and left.

"He's probably wondering what other surprises he'll encounter in married life," Liz said.

"All part of the mystique. We'll be sure to keep him on his toes." Mary Ann flashed her bright smile. "It's better to *keep* husbands surprised. Then you can do what you want."

Liz had stored her dress in one of Sew Welcome's tall closets. Mary Ann brought it out, wrapped in a plastic cover, and sent her to a curtained fitting room used for clothing projects. "If you need help, give a yell."

One glimpse of the dress's delicate lace overlay, and Liz startled at the smile she saw in the mirror. She slipped it over her head, its ivory silkiness floating almost to the floor, then she zipped the back as far up as she could reach.

When she'd chosen this secondhand dress from Retreads, a vintage clothing store located in downtown Pleasant Creek, the local grapevine had gone viral with the news: "The mayor's bride is going to wear a hand-me-down to her wedding!"

Now, as she smoothed its folds before the mirror, Liz affirmed her choice more than ever. The classic A-line skirt enhanced her figure. The V-shaped neckline looked exactly right—not too low, but graceful and flattering. She turned to view the deeper V in the back neckline. A cascade of lace formed a small train that rippled when she moved. Unlike many women, Liz hadn't spent much time dreaming about her wedding dress. The minute she'd tried on this consignment gown, though, she had recognized that she and the dress belonged together.

Mary Ann, waiting outside, finished zipping her and arranged her train with deft hands.

Liz had showed off the dress to the Girls, Miriam, and Ruth before, but as she glided back toward the worktable, they murmured in delight.

"Lovely!"

"That dress is so you!"

"Liz, you're an absolute vision."

"What a sweet *Braut* you will be!" This last from Aunt Ruth, who clasped Liz in a fervent hug as tears slipped down her cheeks. "And Jackson, such a *Bräutigam*! You will have a good life together."

Her aunt's embrace, her friends' loving compliments, the flow of the dress as she walked—all combined to drown out the nastiness of recent events. She had been blessed with a man who surpassed her dreams, and family and friends. That was what she would focus on.

The fragrance of Naomi's cinnamon rolls warming in the microwave reminded her that she'd better change before she ate, to prevent goo from marring the gown's perfection.

"Have you made up your mind about wearing a veil?" Naomi asked as she unzipped the dress.

Liz stepped behind the curtain, then out of the dress. "I'd rather wear flowers in my hair. And I'll wear the locket Jackson gave me for my birthday."

Fun wedding talk, plus Naomi's rolls, sweetened the rest of the evening. By the time everyone left, Liz had mellowed so she thought she might actually sleep.

When she entered her quarters, though, Jackson had joined Steve in watching a movie.

"I'm glad you went to your meeting. You look great, Mom." Her son's voice held a tinge of relief.

"She always looks great." Jackson winked at her again.

Steve gave him a pitying glance. "Boy, are you wrong."

"Quiet, you." Liz grabbed a dishtowel from its hook and threatened to whap him with it. They finished watching the movie together.

"You've yawned four times in the last three minutes." Jackson stood and pulled Liz to her feet. "Walk me to the door. I'll meet you at the police station tomorrow. Nine, right?"

She hadn't asked him to go with her, but oh, how she would welcome his presence. "That will make it so much easier."

"You thought I would let you go alone?" He raised an eyebrow at her. "Of course I'll be there. That's the way it will be from now on. You and me. Always. This thing will work out, Liz. It always does."

Watching him walk in the dreamy light of the old-fashioned streetlamps, she believed it.

Stan's mouth tightened slightly when he saw Jackson with Liz, but he didn't look surprised. He gestured to his coffeepot. "Coffee?"

"Already had mine, thanks." Liz had sampled his toxic brew before, and she didn't feel that courageous this morning.

Jackson, however, accepted a cupful. He and the chief exchanged tidbits about town business as Liz looked around the cramped, dusty office. They'd talked over many details here that had often led to criminals' arrests. She'd never thought she might have to defend her own actions.

The chief cleared his throat. "Well, Liz, there isn't any other way to say this, so I'm going to lay it out on the table. We found brownish dust with small fragments in your inn's kitchen and pantry. I had it tested, and it's ricin."

She gasped, then bit her lip.

Jackson took her hand, then turned to the chief. "Stan, you know perfectly well Liz didn't kill Geoffrey Teal."

"And you know perfectly well I have to do my job, no matter how I feel."

Unfriendly silence, a deep chasm, stretched between the friends.

Liz couldn't bear it. "I-I know you do, Chief."

Dumping more coffee into his mug, Stan shifted the subject. "Earlier I heard about your wedding song, the one you found in your mom's diary."

So he already knew about the composer controversy. "I believe my father wrote it."

"When I called Ms. Watson yesterday, she told me that Teal—Trey Edmond—wrote it. Of course, she didn't want to give me profit figures, but I got it out of her assistant. The song has gone international. It's raking in the royalties."

Liz stared. Jackson's eyes widened.

The chief's heavy brows lowered so Liz couldn't see his eyes. "Hundreds of thousands. Maybe more. When I called this morning, the assistant told me that the minute they posted Edmond's death on their website, sales shot way higher than predicted and were still growing."

Liz couldn't make a sound.

He leaned forward in his squeaky chair. "Liz, are you *sure* you found those lyrics in your mom's diary? Lots of songs sound alike, you know."

"She's sure." Jackson said what Liz couldn't. "Liz gave me a copy of the words, and you can compare them to the radio version."

"I'm sure it's a great song." That gentle tone again. "But Liz, this song authorship business puts you in a tough position. If Teal wasn't your uncle and he stole the song, he was raking in boatloads of money that rightfully belonged to you, with the potential for a lot more."

Motives for murder. The blood seemed to have drained from her body.

"And those deposits—money you said you didn't know about?" His voice was colder. "Some might think those were blackmail payments Teal lined up to keep you quiet, and clearly they didn't accomplish their purpose."

"If it was blackmail money, why would she tell you about it?" Jackson demanded.

Still wordless, Liz shot him a warning glance. *Stop, Jackson. You'll make it worse.*

"I don't know. I don't know a lot of things," the chief continued in the weird, almost monotone voice. "Maybe Liz thought the bank or I would figure out the blackmail factor and wanted to beat us to the draw." He hesitated. "Then there's the assault on Steve—"

"You think I hurt my own son?" Liz barely kept from screeching.

"Of course not." The chief stared at his coffee mug. "But you're a mom. You love that boy more than your life. If Teal attacked him when he stole the diary—your proof of his fraud—for you, that might have been the last straw."

She bolted her gaze to Jackson because she didn't dare look at Stan.

Still, out of the corner of her eye, she saw the chief push back his sparse hair. Then slowly, like an old, old man, he stood, signaling the end of their interview. "We'll have to talk about this further, Liz. Don't leave town."

17

For once, Liz couldn't eat Mary Ann's cherry pie at lunch. For once, Mary Ann didn't insist she try.

While the Material Girls, Steve, and Jackson had huddled in Liz's breakfast nook, she related their meeting with the chief.

Steve's face darkened. He appeared so mad he couldn't speak.

But Liz had never seen such a unanimous deer-in-the-headlights response from the Girls.

In a split second, however, Sadie's morphed to that of a charging moose. She slammed a fist on the table and spewed uncomplimentary adjectives. "What is the *matter* with Stan Houghton? Is he drinking stupid juice or something?"

Maybe the way Steve and the other Girls joined in could be attributed to herd instinct. Liz, her head on the table, didn't care. For a few moments, their wrathful love surrounded her.

"Believe me, I know how you all feel." Jackson, who had jumped to Liz's defense with the chief, now took another approach. "But the chief's just doing his job."

Before Sadie could explode, Jackson continued, "Naturally Stan doesn't think Liz is guilty. But he had to describe the situation as it appears in the eyes of the law. He had to tell it like it is. Whether any of us likes it or not."

Liz raised her head. "You all know Jackson's right."

"But I don't *want* him to be right."

Liz gaped at Naomi, usually the gentle listener.

"I want Houghton to say what he should—that this bizarre idea that you're somehow responsible for Geoffrey's death absolutely, positively can't be true." Her friend's usually sweet eyes glinted dangerously. "And I want someone to pay for this. For hurting Steve. For making you look like a criminal when it should be the happiest time in your life."

A hum of agreement eddied throughout the room. Steve encircled Liz with his arm. "We're all here for you, Mom."

"Thank you." Liz hugged him. "You're all wonderful." Her eyes filled as she looked at her glowering supporters. "You and Jackson make this bearable."

"We're glad to do that." Mary Ann patted her hand. "But let's come up with a plan. Liz, what can we do to help? Is it time to call Nina Davis?"

I hope I don't need a criminal attorney. I wish I knew. She said slowly, "I think all this is connected to Eleanor Watson and Innovation Sounds. Jackson thought we rattled her cage, and I agree. But then the chief called us about Geoffrey and we had to return home. Why would I come back if I was guilty?" Recalling their encounter with Ms. Watson, she spoke through gritted teeth. "If only I could go back to Nashville and dig for the truth."

"I'm glad you can't." Jackson looked her straight in the eye. "I won't have lunatics shooting at you again."

"I'm with Jackson." Steve stuck out his chin. "This is a no-brainer, Mom."

Stubborn, unreasonable men. But how she loved them.

Mary Ann said crisply, "You can't go, Liz. But after the funeral, I'm going to Nashville."

"*We're* going." Sadie crossed her arms. "We can close the shop for a couple of days."

"Sure we can."

"Not on my account, you won't." Liz glared. "I don't have guests coming till next month now. I'll mind your store."

Naomi scanned the calendar on her phone. "No major projects until the weekend. Candice and Jenny can run the bakery while I'm gone."

Opal leafed through her little planner. "I'll get subs to do my Meals on Wheels deliveries this week."

Caitlyn was already on her phone, trading shifts.

The Material Girls threw information back and forth as they talked and phoned.

"It seems," Liz murmured to Jackson, "that I have no input in this."

"Nope. And get used to something else," Jackson said firmly. "My place is right beside you. Just because you're here in Pleasant Creek doesn't mean you're safe. So I'll check in during the day, and at night I'll sleep with Beans."

"He won't like sharing his rug." Liz laughed and hiccuped to cover a sob. She loved these wonderful people so.

The Girls quickly came to a consensus. They would close Sew Welcome and Sweet Everything a little early—around four—and take off by four thirty. Sadie claimed first leg of the journey, driving the Patchwork Bomb.

Liz's phone rang.

"I've been missing you, cousin."

Liz immediately recognized Miriam's calm voice, though to hear it on the telephone was unusual. Her husband, Philip, must have let her use his business phone. "Would you like to come over this evening? If Steve is improved sufficiently, you are welcome to stay the night."

A night at Miriam's peaceful farm. Just the thought soothed Liz's frayed nerves. "Well, I can't stay all night. Steve's not quite—"

"You can't what?" Jackson interrupted. "Stay at Miriam's? It would do you good. I'll stay with Steve."

Do I trust you two? Nevertheless, Liz accepted with gladness. "I'll eat supper with Steve first, so don't add another plate for me. And thanks, Miriam. I can't wait to see you."

"You'll get a real break at Miriam's," Jackson said after she hung up. "But I'd feel better if you don't tell *anyone* you're going there. And take a roundabout route to the farm." He frowned. "Maybe this isn't such a good idea. Will they be able to protect you?"

"They protect themselves well enough. I'm going." She just wanted peace.

Especially since she faced the prospect of Geoffrey's funeral in a few minutes.

"I'll come with you to the funeral home, Mom, if you want me to," Steve said to her amazement.

He was indeed acting more like himself. His tender words made keeping her composure even harder.

Jackson intervened. "I'll be with her, Steve, and so will the Girls."

Liz hugged her son again. "Thanks for thinking of me. But remember what Dr. Sam said: You'll get well faster if you maintain a low-stress lifestyle. You and I both know this doesn't qualify."

"All right," he acquiesced reluctantly.

"I'll be fine. Sarah will be here if you need anything." Liz smoothed her hair in front of a mirror by the back door.

"Okay Mommy," he teased.

She made a face, but blew him a kiss as they left for Yoder Funeral Home, a sedate Victorian house with cheerful pansies and mums decorating its wide front porch.

The simple brass urn and enlargement of Liz's photo of a laughing Geoffrey had been placed on a table, with nearby candles providing soft light. The choking fragrance of too many flowers engulfed the room. They covered the entire front of the chapel.

Standing beside Jackson before the urn, Liz's throat closed so she could hardly breathe. How could such a gifted life be reduced to so little?

When this nightmare ended, she hoped to confirm that he had been a victim more than a predator.

Jackson gently tugged on her elbow, then guided Liz to a seat. On the way, her eyes fell on a showy bouquet from Innovation Sounds. Her stomach lurched.

Had Geoffrey's murderer sent him flowers?

Grief ripped through her, and angry tears that had lurked under cover burst from their hiding place. Jackson leant her his handkerchief and wrapped a comforting arm around her shoulders.

While soft guitar music played through speakers, other mourners gradually filled the chapel to bursting, then stood in the entryway and on the porch. When Liz had calmed herself, she stole glances at the crowd. Had any family shown up? If so, they made no move to identify themselves. Most appeared to be fans from out of town. Liz met the stony stares of a few local devotees, who probably had heard various versions of the case against her.

Not anticipating a big gathering, Mary Ann had helped Tom Yoder plan a simple service, with Pastor Brad reading from the book of Psalms and giving a short eulogy. A small screen displayed brief video excerpts of Geoffrey's more thoughtful songs—*not* including "Love, You Are My Friend"—and fun snapshots Sadie had caught during coffee hour.

Liz tried to focus on Pastor Brad's voice, but she felt an unknown gaze had fastened on her like a leech. With surreptitious shifts in her chair, Liz tried to discover its source. No one appeared to notice her existence.

She'd attended other victims' funerals, paying her respects and often gathering valuable information about family, friends, and enemies.

Now, however, she could not shake the impression that someone was studying her. Had her stalker from Nashville come to Pleasant Creek? Or did he have a counterpart here? Liz tried not to shiver. Or was she simply sensing growing hostility from Trey Edmond's fans?

Jackson seemed to feel what she felt. He stirred uneasily beside her and exchanged glances with Mary Ann on his other side. When the service ended, Jackson and the Girls formed a tight group that quickly escorted Liz outside.

She wanted to accuse them of being overprotective. But if the newly arrived reporters interviewed locals, they would discover the rumors that surrounded Liz.

Jackson and her friends kept Liz in the center of their band until they were safely back at the inn.

After checking on Steve, who was napping, she threw her arms around Jackson, then each of the Girls. "Thanks for helping me escape."

"I think," Jackson said, "that you need a little quiet." He frowned. "I wish I could stay with you all day, but—"

"*Somebody* has to make money." Liz gave him a smile that felt unconvincing even to her.

"Beans will stick with you," Sadie offered.

Liz blinked. The bulldog had left his rug and now stood in front of her, big eyes wide open. They were a soft, gentle brown, something she didn't often see because they were closed 95 percent of the time.

Beans nosed Liz's knee as if to say, "I'm here for you."

Jackson's eyes widened. "I didn't know the old guy had it in him."

Sadie sniffed. "I keep telling you all that Beans is a *very* sensitive dog."

When everyone scattered back to work, Beans followed Liz to the kitchen. He didn't even glance toward his food dish, but sat pressed against Liz's leg as she ate yogurt and an apple. When she took her laptop to the four-season room, he nosed her knee repeatedly, whining.

"What's your problem, Beans?"

He leaped onto the rattan sofa.

She gaped at him. Bean rarely exhibited that much energy. Now he pushed at the laptop as if it were an enemy.

Struggling to hold on, she said, "Beans, do you want me to rest?"

He gave a low woof—and refused to stop pushing until she set it on the floor. Beans leaned against Liz until she hugged his big, furry body.

Okay, okay. Just don't sit on my lap.

It wasn't exactly like snuggling with a warm puppy, as he took up three-fourths of the sofa, but with each moment of his doggy embrace, her contorted heart untwisted a little more.

She lost track of how long they shared a hug on the sofa. She must have dozed off, because when she came to, Beans had climbed down and was sitting, ears erect, by the door to the backyard. Had he stood guard the whole time?

"You sweet boy."

At the sound of her voice, he jumped on the sofa again for another round of hugs. Refreshed more than she'd thought possible, Liz headed for the rotunda. Beans headed for his cherished rug, snoring almost before he hit the floor. Liz patted him. "Good dog."

She found Steve on the front porch, reading. "Glad you got a nap too, Mom. Beans looked like he was guarding Fort Knox. I've never seen him like that."

"It's a rare thing, believe me." Even if the bulldog never reached that level of motivation again, she would forever remember his help today.

Liz summoned enough oomph to go upstairs and touch base with the contractors. They foresaw finishing Jackson's office and man cave within a week. She came back downstairs and did laundry and baked pumpkin bread for guests that would come in handy after she and Jackson returned from their honeymoon. Where were they going?

Jackson had kept their destination secret, telling her only that it would be beautiful, but not fancy.

Thinking of the honeymoon reminded her that she still had some work to do on the reception. She hoped the weather would cooperate, as the reception was meant to take place outdoors. She planned the placement of tables and reviewed food arrangements, complete with sticky notes to remind her of calls she needed to make.

In planning the reception line after the ceremony, Liz saw herself wearing the gown, tiny flowers woven into hair French-braided around her face, her other tresses loose on her shoulders. The pearl-studded locket from Jackson would glow on her neck, but not as brightly as she would. Liz let herself imagine Jackson wearing a navy suit that brought out topaz lights in his hazel eyes and made his thick hair glisten in the sunlight. It would forever be the most precious day of her life.

Liz's daydreams nearly made her late to the Girls' send-off, but she hurried out and made it to the parking lot just as Opal arrived.

Jackson had to work into the evening because he'd spent so much time with her. She smiled gratefully at Steve when he joined her. After the Girls left, she wouldn't be alone.

"I will pray for you. Please stay safe." She hugged each one.

"You too," they all replied. They joined in a prayer, then a silent, teary group hug that lasted too long.

Beep!

They all jumped. Steve, wearing an evil grin, honked the van's horn again. *Beep, beep!*

Steve was indeed acting more like himself.

The Girls yelled and waved as Sadie peeled out of the parking lot.

Steve said, "I need chicken and noodles from Mama's Home Cooking to settle my nerves."

"I could do with a bit of that myself."

It was strange. The feeling of being followed didn't exert itself during dinner at the local restaurant, though plenty of glances, both English and Amish, were aimed Liz's way again. She chose to ignore them and enjoy Mama's succulent chicken and noodles with her son.

As they passed the inn on the way to the parking lot, Steve jolted and pointed to something on the front porch. "Hey, what's that?"

Liz stiffened. "I didn't order anything."

Walking to the porch, Steve looked anything but weak. "Let me check it out first, Mom."

They crept toward the front porch as if expecting an exploding package. Instead, another carefully wrapped bouquet sat before the front door.

"The florist closed at five. Someone else brought these." Liz tried to calm her hammering heart. "Jackson wouldn't send me flowers without telling me beforehand."

"I think the chief should take a look at this."

"You think so?"

"Are you kidding? After the castor bean business?"

Liz gulped. Yet after this morning's session, she was in no hurry to see Stan again. "Why don't we wear gloves and check the card? If it's anonymous or questionable, the bouquet goes downtown." If the flowers turned out to be a gift, well, she could use another day-brightener.

"*You* don't touch them, period." They entered the inn through the back door. Steve donned rubber gloves from Liz's first aid kit and unwrapped the sizable arrangement.

Peach-colored and ivory roses, mingled with lilies. Flowers she planned to use in her wedding decor.

"Oh, my." Liz clasped her hands. Surely the Girls had sent them, since she hadn't even decided on her color scheme until recently. The earlier bouquet had been lovely, but these were positively exquisite.

"They are awfully pretty." He opened the accompanying envelope and held the card so Liz could see it.

May happiness be yours as long as you live.

No signature.

"What's that mean?" Steve demanded. "Is that some kind of a threat?"

"I don't know." Liz pressed her pounding head with both hands. They hadn't come from Geoffrey, so who had sent them?

"One way or another, the chief's going to see it." Before she could say another word, Steve had picked up the bouquet and headed to the parking lot and his car.

The flowers' pretty heads bobbed as he left, pathetic pawns in this ugly game.

Jackson found her sitting on the front porch after Steve left. "What's wrong?"

She told him in a quivering voice.

"You haven't received any more deposits, have you?" he asked, face tight.

"No." She took a shuddering breath. "I hate this. I hate it."

He looked so sad that Liz continued, trying to make him feel better. "I shouldn't make a big deal out of this without knowing more." She straightened. "Hopefully, the Girls will find clues in Nashville. This case has to break soon."

"Even if it doesn't, we're getting married right on schedule." Jackson put his arms around her and held her close.

Steve returned, his face brightening when he saw Jackson. "Stan will check out the flowers and call you."

Nodding, Liz almost wished she could join them this evening.

Still, she needed time with Miriam more than ever. She kissed Jackson good night and gave Steve a hug. "You've had plenty to eat, so try not to empty the fridge," she told him.

He just laughed.

She complied with Jackson's advice to take a different route to Miriam's and arrived safe and sound, confident she had not been followed. Her cousin had lit lanterns on her front porch, and their friendly glow welcomed Liz as if to another time and place, where tranquility reigned. Miriam's smile lit the porch almost as much as the lanterns. Little Keturah bounded down the steps to greet Liz, and her older sister, Grace, handed Liz a mug of hot cider.

The whole family was gathered that evening, so Liz didn't expect that she and Miriam would be able to talk about anything serious. Instead they chatted lightly on the porch while the girls hovered. Because the twilight grew chilly, they soon went inside. Philip, Miriam's husband, had built a small fire, the first of the fall season. He seemed somewhat reserved that evening, disappointing Liz a little—they'd gotten along so well recently.

Still, she enjoyed a highly competitive game of Dutch Blitz with Miriam and the children. Afterward, a protesting Keturah had to go to bed. Grace brought out fabric to practice her sewing by the light of a lantern. Miriam's teen boys planned a fall hunting trip with their father while Liz and Miriam rocked. In the kerosene lamplight, Miriam knit thick socks her sons would need for the coming winter. Liz had brought quilt pieces to hand-sew together to form blocks—a slow process when only lamplight guided her sewing. But this evening was all about slowing her pace and breathing between stitches.

She loved the solemn quiet as Philip read from the Bible before bedtime. The Borkholders also sang a hymn in Swiss that might sound like a dirge to most English ears. But by now, Liz had grown accustomed to the slow, deep music, and its simplicity added to the night's serenity.

A hot shower would have felt good this evening. Washing her hands and face in a tin pan before bed didn't quite cut it. How did large Amish families manage without modern conveniences like indoor plumbing?

Liz soon discovered that she was to stay in the girls' room. When she protested, Miriam answered firmly, "Keturah's in the trundle, and Grace wanted to sleep in front of the fire."

The girl's eager face confirmed her mother's assertion.

Snuggled in their featherbed and quilts, guarded by Keturah's two faceless, Kapped rag dolls on a nearby chair, Liz slept deeper than she had in weeks. When the September sun winked from behind trees, fringing the cornfields, she happily joined in flipping pancakes and homemade sausage patties on their woodstove. She'd thought Miriam's gigantic bowl of batter far too big, but the family soon proved her wrong.

Enjoying her own breakfast, Liz reluctantly planned her day. She should return to the inn well before nine so she could shower and ready Sew Welcome for business. She'd gone off the grid after telling the Girls where she was, but once she left Miriam's, she'd check her phone for word from Nashville. And probably a sweet morning greeting from Jackson. She smiled.

She missed her dishwasher and running water that morning. As she and Miriam pumped water into heavy kettles and lifted them onto the stove to heat, Liz thought that returning to the inn might not prove so difficult, after all.

Keturah helped in cleaning the kitchen more than Liz had expected. They had just hung up dishcloths to dry when Miriam stiffened.

Liz followed her gaze out the front windows. "Is that Bishop Manz talking to Philip?"

Miriam nodded. Her indigo eyes had clouded.

Liz wanted to ask, "What's the matter?" But Keturah and Grace were listening. Hopefully, before Liz left, she'd find out what news had disturbed her cousin.

The men—mostly the bishop—talked briefly. When Philip and Bishop Manz approached the porch, Miriam said, "Grace, Keturah, go make the beds and dust upstairs."

The little girl protested, "But I want to stay with you and Liz."

One look from her mother squelched Keturah's protest, and she followed her sister with the air of a martyr.

Liz would have exchanged a smile with Miriam if her cousin hadn't looked so troubled.

"What's wrong?" Liz clasped her hands.

Miriam's fingers dug into Liz's hands. "Have you packed your belongings?"

Liz blinked. "No, but I can gather everything—"

"Ms. Eckardt." Philip's heavy voice behind them shattered the pleasant morning.

Ms. Eckardt. Not Liz.

As one, she and Miriam turned.

Despite a difference in age, Philip and Bishop Manz, with their iron eyes and faces, could have been twins.

Philip said, "Ms. Eckardt, I am sorry, but you must leave my house. And never come back."

18

Liz tried to move her lips, but they were frozen.

Miriam's voice quivered. "My cousin should know what is held against her, should she not?"

Bishop Manz answered. "She can talk with Chief Houghton, as I have. We shall not discuss such things here."

Last night, Liz had wondered at Philip's renewed reserve. Now his cold voice numbed her very bones as he repeated, "You must leave."

"I'll collect my belongings." Liz hurried upstairs, lest she put Miriam in an even more difficult situation.

She had to go before the girls found out she'd been thrown out. If she saw those sweet faces, she'd burst into tears.

She heard their voices as they cleaned their parents' room, but she packed and sneaked downstairs before they detected her.

Miriam looked at Liz, her eyes dark pools of despair. How Liz longed to ease the pain in her face, which was as white as her bleached apron. She guessed Miriam had been forbidden to speak to her. Liz poured all her love into the gaze she gave Miriam before driving away.

Normally, whys would have swarmed through her mind like angry bees. But today was not a normal day. Liz tried to cry. She couldn't.

Right now, she couldn't talk to anyone, not even Jackson.

Liz returned to the inn and showered. By then, her mouth could move again, so she opened Sew Welcome for business. The needs of a steady stream of customers helped harden the flimsy shell protecting her grief. She didn't remember to check her phone until past ten.

A text reassured her that the Girls had arrived safely in Nashville late last night. This morning, Mary Ann texted that they had just arrived at the Innovation Sounds offices. Liz saw nothing more from them.

Jackson had texted, asking if she'd like to have lunch.

Between the morning's pancakes and the morning's misery, her stomach heaved at the thought of food. But she so wanted to see Jackson.

If only she didn't have to dump another truckload of garbage on him. He probably was feeling more like a trashman than a groom. Nevertheless, during a customer lull, she called and haltingly related what had happened.

Jackson spoke calmly. "Whenever you feel like eating, we'll pick up something. But I'm going to call Stan and demand that he see us. If he won't, we'll park in his waiting room until he does."

"The mayor is proposing a sit-in at the police station?" Only Jackson could restore a splinter of her sense of humor.

"You bet. Make protest signs and meet me there. And wear bell-bottoms."

"Gotcha."

As Liz hung up, she concluded they both had gone insane. But after the past few weeks, who wouldn't?

She finished the morning cutting fabric, selling notions, and smiling at customers. Nothing from Nashville showed up on her phone.

But three nasty, anonymous e-mails scourged her for Trey Edmond's death. More vitriol blazed on the inn's social media page. She deleted them, but figured such hostility would soon overwhelm her social media.

Liz walked downtown, her strides gathering momentum as she returned hellos and ignored probing glances. Would her stalker shadow her today? She didn't care.

Jackson stood in front of the police station, his face like a beacon. She hugged him, then straightened her shoulders. "Let's do this." They marched inside.

Stan stood behind the counter. Most people would not detect any difference in his demeanor, but Liz saw a droop in his eyes and extra lines in his face. He gestured toward his office. "Come on in."

Liz's rickety metal chair rattled as she told him what happened at Miriam's. "The bishop wouldn't tell me what I did. What did he tell you?"

Stan exhaled. "He said he saw you arguing with Geoffrey Teal at the Richards auction."

Liz stared. "The one on Labor Day? I wasn't even there."

"He says you were. So do his wife and three other congregation members who attended the auction, two of whom had seen Teal around town. You and he were quarreling about a song and money. You threatened him."

A song? *Threatened?*

Liz's body wanted to collapse like a rag doll, but she leaned forward, never taking her eyes from his face. "Chief, I don't know what he's talking about. I. Was. Not. There."

He leaned forward too. "Then can you remember where you were about eleven thirty?"

She filed through her mental calendar. "I went for a drive before Jackson picked me up midafternoon and took me to the Wildton festival."

"Was anyone else at the inn when you were there?"

"No, my guests had all left. Sarah had the day off. Mary Ann and Sadie had closed Sew Welcome for the holiday too."

"No mail, so no mail carrier saw you. Anybody else drop by?"

"No, Beans and I were all by ourselves." She was tempted to say, "Ask him," but thought better of it.

The chief's brows lowered. "You went by yourself on that drive?"

"I was trying to get away from it all." *So much for that.*

Stan tore his gaze away and typed on his phone. "Somebody may have seen you go or return, but . . ."

She mentally finished his sentence: Even if they did, she could have driven to the nearby auction.

"I suppose you didn't stop for gas? Or a snack?"

"No. And I didn't drive on the interstate or in Fort Wayne, so no cameras caught me. I stuck to country roads." Now that the shock of the bishop's accusation was wearing off, Liz's anger awakened. "Labor Day was almost two weeks ago. If Bishop Manz was so concerned about my behavior, why didn't he come forward sooner?"

"Apparently, he didn't think it significant. He just saw it as more evidence of English depravity, I guess." A ghost of a smile tugged at Stan's mouth, then quickly vanished. "People don't gossip much with a bishop, and Teal was an outsider, far removed from his circle. So the bishop didn't learn of his death until two days ago. After talking with the others who'd attended the auction, he put two and two together." The chief shook his head. "Your staying with the Borkholders must have been the last straw. The bishop had to protect his flock at all costs."

His flock. That included Aunt Ruth and Uncle Amos and their children and grandchildren. All the precious family members she'd come to love. The ones for whom she'd made the move to Indiana.

Liz felt Jackson's arm around her, but she didn't dare look at him or she'd fall apart right there.

He said hoarsely, "The bishop obviously mistook someone else for Liz."

"That would be my theory," the chief said, "except that it wasn't just his account. I've talked individually with the others—solid people, not troublemakers—who have seen Liz plenty of times around town and at her relatives'. Their accounts match Bishop Manz's." He looked away, knuckles whitening as he gripped the edge of his desk. "The women even described the outfit you're wearing today, including that scarf. Accurately."

Liz's hand went to her neck. "My scarf? They described my *scarf*?"

Her charcoal pants and blue T-shirt—that could have been coincidental. Any stranger could have worn those solids. But the scarf, with its blue, gray, and purple geometric pattern?

He nodded.

She was speechless.

Jackson wasn't. "I don't care what they said or what they think they saw," he snapped, his eyes flashing. "You know and I know, Stan, that if Liz says she didn't do something, she didn't do it." He leaned forward and glared into the chief's face. "Are you charging her with anything?"

She waited. Would she be jailed before her wedding day?

After what seemed like hours, the chief shook his head.

"Then we're leaving. Now." He pulled Liz to her feet and stomped to the empty reception area and out the door.

Jackson was breathing hard, and his expression alarmed her. Liz said, "Want to go for a walk around the lake?"

He spat out, "Before we walk a block, somebody will stop us and want to gossip."

She decided not to reply.

Her going for a drive on Labor Day certainly had complicated her life. And she couldn't venture far from Pleasant Creek, per the chief's directive. So she coaxed, "Want to take a little ride? I'll drive."

"Okay." He muttered. "Probably safer for both of us."

They hurried to the town parking lot and climbed into his truck. Once out of town, Liz pushed the truck past speed limits as they roared down country roads. They opened all the windows, the wind wreaking joyous havoc with Liz's hair. For some minutes, neither said anything. They simply gulped in the golden afternoon as if it were an antidote.

Finally, Jackson said, "I don't know how you can stay calm."

"I don't know either," she said truthfully.

She thought of turning toward the Amish schoolhouse. They'd see the children, always darling in their black outfits, walking home from school. She might catch a glimpse of Keturah and Grace. Though she'd seen them only this morning, her eyes filled with tears.

Liz turned in the opposite direction.

They took a favorite route near River Road and the covered bridge, where they decided to stop.

"Wish I had my fishing pole," Jackson said, sounding less angry.

She wished he did too. Liz wished they could wander here forever, listening to their footsteps echo throughout the venerable wooden bridge, floating autumn-tipped leaves in the meandering green river, holding hands, smiling at each other—

River Road.

The words strangled each other.

The police had found Geoffrey's body near here.

Jackson looked up as if she'd spoken. His hand tightened around hers. His other hand clenched. He knew.

After a long silence, Jackson said, "Should we go back to the truck?"

"Why?" She choked on the word. "Geoffrey's death will just follow us there."

Jackson's phone rang. He glanced at it, then at Liz. "Mary Ann. I totally forgot to ask if you'd heard from her."

"I haven't checked for hours." Pushing back her messy hair, Liz pulled out her phone.

He took the call. "Hi, Mary Ann. Yes, she's here with me. It's been a rough day."

While he summarized their morning, Liz scanned her texts and messages. *Oh my.*

"Let me talk to her!"

Jackson put his phone on speaker and handed it to her.

"Have you two decided to behave?" Her friend's no-nonsense voice sang sweetly in Liz's ears. "Here we are, doing a serious investigation, and you—"

"They packed up and left?" Liz interrupted.

"Yes, apparently, Innovation Sounds has vanished." Mary Ann's voice held more than a note of triumph. "The door was locked and there was nobody around. The building's manager gave us the runaround, of course. But Sadie found Leona, her janitor friend, and she said last Tuesday night, when she was cleaning carpets, they were carrying boxes and crates out of the office. When she told the building manager the next morning that she thought they were moving out, he hadn't a clue."

Tuesday night. One day after she, Jackson, and Sadie had invaded the office.

"The janitor wouldn't let us go inside, but she let us peek from the door while she walked through the whole office. Empty. You would have thought it had been that way for months."

If that didn't indicate underhanded activity, nothing would. A small candle of hope lit inside Liz. She saw a similar flame illuminate Jackson's eyes.

Mary Ann went on, "We talked to Officer Matthews—you know, the patrolman you met here? He said he'd initially bowed to his superior's focus on Lake Carson as the intended victim, subtly implying that Detective Hawkins craved publicity in order to climb the police department's ladder."

"What else did he say?" Liz was eager for details.

"I'm getting to that," Mary Ann said kindly. "Matthews also said that after reexamining the crime scene and studying ballistics reports, he'd noticed that one shot, supposedly aimed at Lake Carson, had ricocheted off a nearby trash can to hit the brick wall. The straight-on entry angles of the bullets that struck near you and Sadie suggested they'd nearly hit their targets. But the other two shots' angles of entry into the brick wall behind Lake, plus their spent cartridge positions, suggested they might have missed their target by wide margins, rather than narrow."

Sadie broke in. "Officer Matthews thought the gunman might have shot them as he ran away."

In other words, the shots supposedly meant for Lake had been targeted at Liz and Sadie. Liz tried to stifle her rising excitement. Those details didn't prove the officer's scenario, but they, plus the Girls' report about Innovation Sounds, raised enough red flags in Matthews's mind to discuss the case tomorrow with Detective Hawkins.

They had asked the officer to call Stan before he talked with the detective.

"I don't know about that." Liz told Mary Ann about Bishop Manz's statement.

"That old *windbag*!" Sadie exploded in the background. "Does he think all English look alike?"

"Quiet, Sadie," her partner ordered. "Or I'll take us off speakerphone."

Laughter and muttering in the background.

Liz grinned at Jackson. So good to hear normal.

Mary Ann resumed their conversation. "Liz, our evidence won't overturn the bishop's testimony, or those of the others. They're people of integrity who are trying to do the right thing."

Of course, they were. Despite her anger, Liz had never doubted that.

"But I think our findings will help support what the chief believes in his heart, what we all believe: that you're innocent of any wrongdoing, and someone—probably Eleanor Watson—is trying very hard to frame you."

Mary Ann's faith in Stan was confirmed when they returned to the police station and told the chief about the phone call.

He'd already talked to Officer Matthews and Detective Hawkins.

The detective had proven less resistant to their hypothesis when the chief connected the Nashville shooting to Trey Edmond and his now very public death. Even now, Hawkins was tracking down Watson and company. He also was working to obtain a warrant to treat the Innovation Sounds office as a related crime scene.

The chief poured himself a mugful of noxious coffee after Liz's usual polite refusal. "Well, I hope this takes some of the pressure off you."

This time, his fatherly tones didn't irritate her in the least.

The chief lowered his voice and his chin. "I never did believe you killed Teal."

She whispered, "I know."

"But somebody did. Maybe Eleanor Watson. And she's trying very hard to take you out of the picture."

19

"I love Pleasant Creek, but it feels good to cross two whole county lines." Though she savored her freedom, Liz wanted the Acura's windows closed on this drive to preserve her hairstyle.

The chief had lifted Liz's travel ban, and she now drove them to Earth's Bountiful Table, the restaurant Vanessa had recommended.

"Glad we're not waiting till after our wedding to use the gift certificate," Jackson had agreed. "We need the break."

"That should be it." Liz pointed. "I've wanted to try this place for ages."

"We're on a waiting list for a table near the fall flower gardens," Jackson said as they turned into the driveway. "Since it's Saturday, the hostess couldn't make any promises."

"I don't care, as long as nobody knows us."

"Works for me too."

The lot looked full. Liz had to park near the employees' area. Jackson opened her door with a flourish.

The restaurant, housed in an enormous old farmhouse, exuded exactly the charm Liz needed—homey, with background music calculated to soothe the soul.

The entryway, accented by antiques and fresh mums, offered a pleasant wait while the hostess checked garden-view table availability.

Jackson startled.

"What's the matter?" She peered in the direction he indicated, to a side sunroom that housed several tables.

Liz blinked. Her mirror image sat at one of them, wearing a lace-trimmed navy top that resembled one of hers.

Jackson whispered hoarsely, "If I weren't standing beside you, I'd swear that was you."

"Dead ringer," agreed the old gentleman behind them. "She's not your twin?"

"They say everyone has one." Edging closer, Liz frowned. "But that—that's Vanessa. She's wearing a wig. And that makeup is amazing."

Jackson's eyes widened. "Why would she try to look like you?"

"Maybe this is the second time she's done it." Liz tugged him into a corner where they could still see the sunroom through its windows, but also conceal themselves. "Vanessa doesn't appear to have seen us. Let's keep it that way."

"Good idea." Jackson pressed himself farther into the corner. "Who's with her?"

"I don't know. But something about her . . ."

Someone had described a similar elderly lady to Liz. One with lavender-tinted gray hair and a tasteful, designer outfit.

"I've got it." Liz snapped her fingers. "Nadine."

Jackson quirked an eyebrow. "Nadine who?"

"The server at the Amishland Restaurant. She said an older, classy-looking woman had asked about me." Right now, though, the woman didn't look classy, but ill. "Why is Vanessa hauling her to her feet?"

"Poor lady looks like she should stay put," Jackson agreed.

Liz grabbed his arm. "They're coming this way."

Where to hide? They'd never make it to the car before Vanessa and the woman exited.

A raucous group partied at the far end of the restaurant's wraparound porch. When Liz and Jackson joined them, nobody appeared concerned.

"Sit, or you'll stick out." Liz slid into a chair facing away from the entrance. Jackson followed suit.

A few minutes later, Liz sneaked a glance at the Lavender Lady sitting in the passenger side of a silver Lexus. Her head was thrown back, her face bluish gray. Was she breathing?

There was no sign of Vanessa.

Jackson leaped to his feet at the same time Liz did. Before they reached the car, though, a middle-aged woman banged on the Lavender Lady's window. When the passenger didn't move, she yelled, "I'm a nurse. Are you all right, ma'am?" then tried the door. It was unlocked. The rescuer checked a vein in the woman's neck. She pulled out a phone and called 911.

"She's got this, thank God." Liz slowed and scanned the parking lot. "Do you see Vanessa?"

"Not right off."

The grinding of gravel sent them hurrying to the employees' parking area. Liz remembered Vanessa's late-model blue Toyota. Having found the exit, she swerved onto a road behind the restaurant.

Their own spot turned out to be an advantage. Liz started the car and the pursuit almost before Jackson shut his door. With the sunset still in progress, she could see the Toyota turn onto the highway and head for the interstate. "She'll probably take the closest ramp."

"That's what I'd do if I was trying shake someone." Jackson locked his gaze ahead.

May the best woman win. Liz smiled grimly as she zipped the Acura up the ramp and powered into traffic.

Jackson took her nature-watching binoculars from the glove compartment and focused them ahead. "Yeah, she's there, but she's well ahead of us."

"Hopefully, she'll stay on the interstate." Liz glanced at her speedometer. Eighty. Would she get away with going eighty-five?

"By the way, why exactly are we chasing Vanessa?"

Liz cast a reproachful look at his wry half-grin. "You don't trust my gut feeling?"

"Actually, I do. Especially since it matches mine." The levity faded from his voice. "But let's lay out reasons to tell the police when they catch up with us. Because they will." He peered ahead with the binoculars. "Vanessa's passing more cars."

Liz passed an RV. "For starters, she left a helpless elderly woman alone in a parking lot."

"True, but probably not illegal. The old lady may have told her, 'I'm fine, dear. You go ahead home.'"

"Maybe." She zoomed past a row of drivers who respected the speed limit. "But I think Vanessa deliberately impersonated me at that auction to cast suspicion on me as Geoffrey's killer. Which makes me think that she's Eleanor Watson's Pleasant Creek counterpart or, at least, that they're connected in this case." She pounded the steering wheel. "Why didn't I see it? She found out all about the song while she was staying at the inn. I'm thinking that she was the brains behind this, keeping tabs on Geoffrey. And she soon became familiar with my style."

"Now Vanessa's done the impersonation thing again with this old lady. Any idea why?" Jackson's fingers drummed the seat.

"I haven't a clue." The poor woman. Would she be all right?

Jackson said, "It's all so complicated that I don't think police in this county would understand. Shouldn't we call Stan?"

She sighed. "I think we should try to find some answers first. Right now, all I can do is make guesses and whine about Vanessa's stealing my style."

Jackson stiffened. "She's taking the next exit!"

Liz floored it, and they shot past a line of semis. Swerving into the right lane, she veered onto the ramp just in time.

Gripping his seat, Jackson yelled, "Turn right at the stop sign!"

She whipped the Acura onto the deserted rural highway and accelerated. "You don't have to shout."

"Sorry." He exhaled. "Adrenaline rush."

That was his diplomatic version of "fearing for my life."

Liz craned her neck. "Can you see her?"

He held up the binoculars again. "Yeah, she's really moving. I'm surprised the cops haven't chased us." He frowned at the dashboard. "The GPS is just sitting there. Says we're still back at the restaurant."

"Recalculating," said Lavinia.

So the GPS was throwing one of her frequent little fits. At the worst time possible, as the sky grew darker by the moment.

Jackson pulled out his phone. "I only have one bar, so mine's not much better." Holding up the binoculars again, he strained forward. "Can barely see her taillights. If those are hers."

"I hope she hasn't turned off onto a country road." Twists, turns, tractor-sized potholes—Liz didn't relish the prospect.

Neither did Jackson. "I could drive the roads at home with my eyes closed. But I don't know this county well."

"Fortunately, Vanessa probably doesn't either, since she's from Lansing." Liz grimaced. "*If* she's from Lansing."

Jackson said, "I imagine there's a lot we don't know about Ms. Vanessa."

"Is finding out worth the trouble?" At best, they would pay hefty fines for this crazy chase. At worst? Liz didn't want to think about it.

"It's worth it." Jackson's confidence made her dig deep.

Gradually, Liz gained on the taillights. They didn't slow when a small town's lights twinkled on the dark horizon, a confirmation they were on the right track. Who else would zoom through Maypole, Indiana, at seventy miles an hour?

Liz struggled to keep up. "Let's hope nobody's standing in the middle of the road talking corn prices."

Fortunately, the town appeared to have rolled up its sidewalks, and they barreled through without incident. Several miles down the road, though, when Liz had pulled within five car lengths, a siren's faint wail pierced the air.

Vanessa's tires screeched as she turned down a side road. Liz's sang a similar discord as she wrenched the Acura's steering wheel to the right and roared after her.

"Probably the sheriff." Jackson peered out the back window. "No flashing lights yet. But they'll come."

Liz saw no reason to hold back now. "I have to catch that car."

She pushed the Acura to its limits, barely holding the road's curves. Liz pulled up beside the Toyota on the somewhat narrow road that now straightened into a drag racer's dream. Liz edged closer to Vanessa's car until she could see the woman's profile hunched over the wheel...

Bump! The impact jolted Jackson as Vanessa banged her car against his side.

Liz wrenched the wheel to keep from swerving off the road, then returned the bump. "Sorry Jackson!"

"I'm all right. Hit her again!"

Liz slowed slightly, then slammed her right headlight into the Toyota. Vanessa's car veered into a ditch. Liz fought to maintain control, finally braking to the side of the road. "Jackson, are you hurt?"

"My door's jammed. Open yours and let's catch her. She's running!"

Liz jumped out. He was right behind her. Sirens screamed as they flipped on the flashlights on their phones and dashed madly across the harvested soybean field.

One moment, Jackson, with his long legs, was quickly closing the gap between himself and Vanessa. The next, she vanished.

He halted, gasping. "Where'd she go?"

Liz desperately scanned the dark landscape with her flashlight. "There's a barn over that rise. She's probably hiding there."

"Or she may have headed for the woods behind it." He took off again. Liz was several yards behind, but was thankful she'd worked to keep in shape for her wedding dress.

With all the hiding places the nearby forest offered, they could chase Vanessa all night and not catch her.

More sirens. *Please let us catch her before they catch us.*

They topped the rise. No sign of Vanessa. Only a combine parked next to the barn.

It suddenly roared to life.

They froze.

The huge machine lurched forward, then sped up, headlights shining like some nocturnal monster's eyes.

Grabbing her hand, Jackson dragged Liz away.

"Run ahead! Don't worry about me!" She was gasping now, as the combine gobbled up the distance between them faster than she'd ever imagined. "Call Stan!"

Shots rang out.

Now Liz ran faster than she'd ever imagined.

"Head for the woods!" Jackson cried.

The combine, with its giant, crushing tires, thundered on their heels, and the woods seemed no closer. Liz prayed aloud as she ran. *What a weird way to die*, remarked some disconnected part of her mind.

Huge lights blinded her. She stumbled and fell.

"Stop!" A man's voice yelled. "You on the combine, stop now or I'll shoot."

The monster's thunder faded to a rumble, then died.

Jackson crouched beside her. "Liz. Liz." He drew her to him.

"Don't move," another voice growled. The excruciating light blurred everything in its painful halo. Liz could see very little.

Well enough, however, to make out the silhouette of a gun pointing at them.

20

Shielding her eyes with her hands, Liz could barely make out sheriffs' uniforms.

Hands raised, Jackson nodded toward Vanessa, who was climbing out of the combine at gunpoint. "That woman was trying to kill us. We were lucky to escape with our lives."

Still gasping, Liz couldn't speak. She glanced sideways at their pursuer. Vanessa's silhouette portrayed her usual short haircut. Where was her wig?

Mercifully, the light dimmed somewhat.

"These maniacs pursued me for miles," Vanessa accused. "They rammed my car, ran me off the road, and then chased me all over the field." She pointed back at the road. "Look at my Toyota, if you don't believe me."

"Look at my Acura!" Liz retorted.

"But you're the one who took off in my combine." A new figure had appeared, a stocky one wearing a baseball cap and carrying a rifle.

"You shot at me!" Vanessa cried.

"Yep, I got a thing about people who take what doesn't belong to 'em. What in blue blazes were you doin' on my combine?"

"Quiet, all of you." The stern voice of the tall man—he must be the sheriff—brooked no argument.

But Vanessa wasn't done. "This woman has harassed me beyond belief, despite my helping her after her son's hospitalization. If I hadn't scared them off with the combine, they would have done me in."

Vanessa sounded downright righteous, with a womanly touch of pathos.

"Who would have done whom in?" Jackson spat.

"I'm not even going to try to straighten this out here. You're all coming to the station." The sheriff barked into his walkie-talkie, then turned to the farmer. "Charlie, you too. But you can follow us there."

The sheriff grunted to two deputies, who confiscated phones and handcuffed Liz, Jackson, and Vanessa. For once, Liz gave thanks that her mother could not see her bound like a criminal and shoved into a police car. And that all Pleasant Creek wasn't witnessing their humiliation.

Not yet, anyway.

Jackson didn't mention he was a mayor, probably because the sheriff wouldn't believe him. At this point, he wouldn't believe anything they said, so Liz held her peace.

Thankfully, when Jackson requested that he and Liz ride together, the sheriff permitted it—mostly to separate them from Vanessa. Jackson couldn't hold Liz's hand, but his presence made this appalling scenario bearable.

But for how long?

Not long enough. When they arrived at the tiny police station, the sheriff took Jackson into a side room and closed the door.

When would she see him again?

Liz tried to hold back tears as a deputy guided her into another room, hardly bigger than a closet. Vanessa, remaining in the outer office with an officer, smirked at Liz before the door closed.

Big mistake, lady. Liz straightened. She would cooperate and try to present their case in the sanest possible way.

When the deputy questioned her, she gave precise answers, emphasizing that they thought Vanessa had harmed the elderly woman at the restaurant. When he asked her why they hadn't called the police, Liz answered truthfully that they weren't at all sure about the situation and didn't want to wrongfully accuse anyone.

"Yet you and your boyfriend chased her halfway across the county and rammed her car?"

"Actually, she rammed mine first."

"All this because you thought she'd hurt an old lady, but you weren't sure?" The man fixed cynical eyes on her. "There's gotta be a lot more to this than you're telling me."

There is, but you wouldn't believe it. Burglary, assault, fraud, possible murder—Liz still wasn't sure of the overall situation, but she knew Vanessa played a major role.

Instead of blurting her suspicions, Liz asked if the elderly woman was all right.

"Pretty sick, the docs say. Haven't heard anymore."

The deputy tapped his keyboard again, then asked, "Is that gal out front after your boyfriend?"

Liz almost laughed. "No. Whatever else Vanessa has done, she hasn't tried to steal my fiancé."

"Fiancé, huh? I can think of better ways to spend a Saturday night with a fiancé than chasing people around a soybean field."

"So can I," Liz said tiredly.

While he tapped away, she considered urging him to call Stan. But the chief knew nothing about Vanessa's part in all this. Liz herself had been jolted only hours before by the "respectable" saleswoman's actions. Should she call Stan before she had a chance to think this through?

Would they even allow her to call him?

The deputy received a text, and his eyes narrowed. "Now, this is interesting. Your 'friend' out front says she didn't have anything to do with the old woman's sickness, that she ate dinner at the restaurant alone. She claims *you* were sitting with the old lady. A server and a customer, after looking at your picture, say it was you too."

Liz groaned. If she and Jackson could hardly believe the weird twists and turns of this case, how could they expect these officers to buy their story?

Yet there seemed no other way.

First, though, she handed the deputy Stan's phone number. "Chief Stan Houghton of the Pleasant Creek police force is a close friend of Jackson's and mine. Jackson happens to be the town's mayor."

The deputy squinted at her.

Liz pushed on. "After hearing my story, perhaps you'll want to call the chief. Or let me call him."

He grunted. "We'll see."

She told him about the burglaries. About the fraud surrounding her family's song. About the shots in Nashville. About Geoffrey's death. About Vanessa's impersonating her before an Amish bishop and in the restaurant.

Liz paused occasionally, hoping for some sign of affirmation.

Eventually, she hoped he might blink.

He only stared as if she had sprouted antennae.

When she finished, he asked if she wanted coffee. She asked if she could have something, anything to eat, since they'd missed dinner.

"I'll have to check with the sheriff."

The deputy left her in the cramped room, locking it behind him. *Is this what it's like to be in jail?*

She hoped she'd never find out.

But when the deputy took her fingerprints and a mug shot, then handed her a garish orange jumpsuit, that hope died.

No sign of Jackson. Her knees wobbled.

"What is the charge?" Liz asked, trying to summon her lawyer voice.

"Speeding, public endangerment, trespassing, disturbing the peace—and attempted murder."

Attempted murder? The words struck her in the chest like a fist.

She couldn't speak, couldn't breathe as he opened a thick steel door and guided her toward the first of two barred cells.

Vanessa eyed her with a sneer from one of them. "Well, well. Liz has come to my pajama party. We're going to have a good time tonight, aren't we?"

She bore the same features of the sweet guest who'd stayed in the Olde Mansion Inn, yet a different person gloated from those narrowed blue eyes.

Liz turned her back on the woman and sat on the narrow cot.

The deputy left a convenience-store sandwich and chips beside her, then slammed the door.

Liz didn't want to give Vanessa additional fodder for tormenting her, but she had to ask the deputy. "Murder? But I didn't hurt anyone."

"You want me to explain it to you?" The man's face hardened. "Witnesses saw you eating with that old lady at the restaurant. The hospital docs say she was poisoned, and she's critical." He glared at her. "You'd better hope she doesn't die."

21

Liz lay on the cell's cot, not unlike a cement slab. She closed her eyes, trying to escape the naked lightbulb outside her cell.

Vanessa, after hours of verbal jabbing and stabbing—and random banging on cell bars— had finally slept, head pillowed on her arm in an almost childlike pose.

But Liz's mind had become her worst enemy. Silent taunts flew at her like spears.

What had become of Jackson? They must have jailed him too, or he would have summoned a dozen lawyer friends, demanding they free her. For once, mayoral credentials hadn't made a difference. Jackson's charm hadn't worked.

She could bear unjust accusations and this rotten cell. She could even endure the prospect of serving extended jail time, if only they could be together.

Their wedding was to take place in less than two weeks. Instead, they might see each other only across a courtroom.

Not satisfied with wringing her heart, Liz's mind reproached her for her blindness. Sure, the clues that pointed to Vanessa hadn't raised red flags. But she should have known that even pink flags sometimes led to truth.

Vanessa had been there. That summarized the evidence against her in a sentence.

A guest at the inn, she'd heard the diary details about "Love, You Are My Friend."

She'd been around when the burglaries took place. Not that she'd knocked Steve unconscious—that wasn't her style. More likely, Vanessa had directed Geoffrey, the tae kwon do enthusiast, to do it and had monitored the situation.

She could have poisoned the bread while "helping" in the kitchen. The poison surely came from the plant Geoffrey gave Liz—a plant from which Vanessa must have harvested bean pods before Liz put it into her own quarters.

While clearing up breakfast, she could have overheard their Nashville plans and warned Innovation Sounds of their imminent arrival.

In observing Liz, Vanessa had effectively copied her style. Approximately Liz's build, with a wig and expert makeup job, she had pulled off the impersonation. Liz kicked herself. Why hadn't she asked the police to look for Vanessa's wig? In her hurry, the woman had probably stashed it in the barn.

She shot a glance at innocent-looking Vanessa, still asleep.

Obviously, if Geoffrey had masterminded this scheme, either she or Eleanor Watson had rebelled and won.

If Liz were a gambler, she'd lay money on Vanessa. Dramatic women like Eleanor Watson couldn't hide. Liz, herself, had likened the CEO in Nashville to a movie villainess. A cartoon. In reality, she probably had been manipulated by someone stronger and more evil. After all, who had fled, and who had remained behind, still wreaking havoc?

But women like Vanessa could operate effectively in the background to ruin lives.

Liz shivered as rage devoured her . . .

But rage did no good. If Vanessa were awake, she'd love it. That last thought, cold and clear, cooled Liz's fury. Gradually, with the help of deep breaths and deeper conviction, she relaxed. Her friends would come.

Wearily, she turned over. For now, she may as well plan on sleeping in.

Wham!

A growl accompanied the door slam. Liz lifted her foggy head from the flat pillow. She didn't remember letting Beans into her quarters.

With the clang of the barred door, she realized where she was. Vanessa growled and swore from the other cell.

However, Liz quickly forgot about that. Chief Houghton, in all his glory, stood before her.

She must be dreaming. Surely, she was dreaming.

But the "phantom" bent and enclosed her in a very real bear hug. "Liz. I should never have let you out of the county."

"No, you shouldn't have," she said, with a chuckle that quickly turned into a sob.

"You *really* shouldn't have." Vanessa sounded like a librarian shushing noisy boys. "Your little Nancy Drew's got herself into big trouble. Even your pulling strings won't help."

Stan glared at Vanessa through the bars. "I won't bother telling you what I've found out. But think about this: Your clothes will be tested for ricin."

With one foot, he pushed Liz's cell door wide open. "Let's go."

He didn't have to say it twice. She restricted her gloating to a mere glance at Vanessa and followed him into the dingy hallway. The deputy who had questioned her the night before avoided Liz's gaze as he opened the steel door.

She fairly skipped through.

Jackson!

Her feet left the floor as he picked her up and spun her around, then kissed her.

"Yeah, because *he* did so much, locked up in a cell just like you were."

Sadie's blunt line cracked them up just before Steve and the Material Girls rushed them.

With all the weeping, laughing, hugging, and explaining, the laconic sheriff only retained Liz and Jackson long enough for a request for them to return later for debriefing.

"How is the lady in the hospital?" Liz asked anxiously.

The sheriff raised an eyebrow. "She's been downgraded to serious. Still real sick, but better."

"Good." Liz hurried to change out of the horrible orange jumpsuit and back into her own clothes.

Agreeing that this day deserved the biggest Sunday brunch ever, they all burst through the police station doors, jammed into the Sew Welcome van, and used GPS to track down the nearest restaurant.

The Country Cookin' Buffet just outside Maypole rivaled any brunch they had sampled. Roast beef and ham, as well as omelets, crepes, breakfast meats, and dozens of other items, loaded the tables.

Liz hadn't been able to stomach much of the jailhouse's soggy egg salad sandwich, so now she ate almost as much as Jackson, wedding dress or not.

Stan pushed back his empty plate with a sigh of satisfaction. "Just wanted you and Jackson to know that the police here aren't going to charge you with anything but speeding."

That sounded way better than the charges that had been listed the night before.

The chief went on, "If that farmer hadn't found that devil woman's wig in his goat feed right away, I doubt we could have sprung you this fast. For the sheriff, I think that was the first hint you hadn't made this whole thing up. That, and Vanessa's fingerprints told him she's been convicted of forgery and fraud in Tennessee."

"I didn't think of asking them to look for the wig until we'd already been jailed. I don't think they knew whether to arrest us or take us to the hospital for psychological tests."

"Thank goodness the farmer found it before the goats did," Mary Ann said. "They'll eat anything."

Steve, on Liz's other side, leaned his head against hers. "Thank God you're safe, Mom."

She soaked in his comfort and silently agreed with all her heart.

Steve, being Steve, soon straightened. "So the sheriff decided to call the chief *after* finding the wig?"

"Yep." Stan sipped his ever-present coffee. "Before that, the police had assumed Liz and Vanessa were the same person, seen by witnesses both in the entry and at the table with Pauline Terrell, the sick lady. But after a busboy had cleaned tables near Vanessa and Mrs. Terrell, he'd exited through the front door to pick up trash in the parking lot, and he saw Liz in the entry. At first he thought you and Vanessa were twins, but then he remembered that Vanessa was wearing tons of makeup, and 'the one in the entry was younger. Prettier.'"

"I could have told them that." Jackson kissed Liz's cheek.

"Then an older man who'd stood behind you two in the entry confirmed the kid's story. The busboy also saw Vanessa sprinkle something on Mrs. Terrell's food while she was in the restroom. He thought it was medicine. When an ambulance came for her, though, the kid worried. He was glad to tell the police when they questioned him."

"I hope the sheriff will give us his name so we can thank him." Liz said. "But does anyone know why Vanessa targeted Mrs. Terrell? She's hardly an up-and-coming musician. And I can't imagine she's in league with Vanessa." She shuddered.

"They'll figure that out when she's better," the chief answered.

"The sheriff ID'd her by her driver's license, and they're trying to find her relatives."

Liz turned to Jackson. "Maybe we can check with the hospital to see if visitors are permitted. I can't imagine being so ill in a strange town without family or friends."

"Hey, I didn't tell you the rest of the story," the chief broke in.

"What 'rest of the story'?" Liz perked up her ears.

"When the sheriff called, I'd just heard from Detective Hawkins in Tennessee."

"That guy who's out to make a name for himself?" Sadie sniffed. "I liked Officer Matthews lots better."

"Yeah, Hawkins has ego, but he does get things done. They caught Ms. Watson's assistant, Stephanie Enders."

Ah yes, the Sweet Dragon. Liz remembered her well.

He continued, "Enders told Hawkins that Watson collaborated with Vanessa to steal music rights from a number of musicians. Enders couldn't stand Vanessa, who often showed up to order them around. Said she'd manipulated and threatened Trey." The chief set his jaw. "I imagine before long we'll uncover additional evidence that Vanessa killed him."

"How could a human being do what she's done?" Naomi pushed away her last cherry crepe.

"We've probably only seen the tip of the iceberg." The chief shook his head.

"Let's talk about something happier!" Caitlyn raised her coffee mug. "I say we toast the upcoming wedding!"

"Hear, hear!"

"Here's to Liz and Jackson!"

They all clinked mugs and applauded.

After the toast, Caitlyn tapped her mug with a spoon, followed by the rest.

Despite the other diners in the room, Liz and Jackson were happy to oblige them with a long, Hollywood kiss.

As the roomful of onlookers applauded, Jackson whispered in Liz's ear, "See, I told you it would all work out."

"Am I in for a lifetime of 'I told you so'?" she asked.

"Maybe." He grinned. "Depends on how often you argue with me."

22

"It's finished!" Liz clapped her hands. "Oh, Girls, it's beautiful!"

Opal finished pressing the Double Wedding Ring quilt, then handed one end to Mary Ann. They stretched it between them, with Sadie taking close-up photos of the quilt and Liz admiring it. Then Caitlyn enlisted Steve to take pictures of the Material Girls standing in front of the quilt.

Liz ran her fingers over the fine stitching. "Thank you all. This is so lovely. I'll want to hang it on the wall instead of putting in on the bed."

"You'd better not." Sadie shook a finger in her face. "We made sure the fabrics are colorfast and won't wrinkle."

"You talked me into it."

The construction crew had completed Jackson's office and his man cave too. It was such a relief to be able to hear herself think again.

Despite unfinished wedding details, she and Jackson drove to Maypole that evening. Liz wanted to visit Mrs. Terrell who, according to the nursing staff, had improved considerably, but remained alone.

A nurse brightened when they asked for directions to her room. "Mrs. Terrell's only visitors have been the police."

They hurried to room 216, knocked, and opened the door a crack.

"Mrs. Terrell?" Liz called. "It's Liz Eckardt and Jackson Cross from Pleasant Creek. Do you mind if we visit for a few minutes?"

"No, I don't mind at all." A woman's voice answered, a Southern accent softening her hoarseness. "Please come in."

They entered the pristine but bare hospital room. Mrs. Terrell, her lavender hair beautifully coiffed, lay in the upright hospital bed.

Large brown eyes filled her pale face. "How kind of you to come see me. Honey, you're pretty as a summer morning."

"Um, thank you." Liz quailed under the intense stare.

"Yes, isn't she?" Jackson shook the woman's hand gently. "We're getting married soon."

"So I heard." Mrs. Terrell dabbed at her eyes with a tissue.

Some people did get emotional about weddings in general. Liz remembered Nadine's comment that the elderly lady had displayed considerable enthusiasm about their nuptials.

Now Mrs. Terrell's eager smile contrasted with her frail body. "Are y'all getting married in a church?"

"Yes. Our church, Pleasant Creek Community," Liz answered.

"I'm so glad to hear that." The woman beamed. "A foundation of faith makes all the difference in a marriage."

Soon she and Liz were discussing her dress, their attendants, and the wedding's color scheme. Jackson teased them mercilessly, and Mrs. Terrell appeared to love every moment.

She was a widow who lived in Louisville with a poodle named Sleepy, the laziest dog in the world. Jackson claimed he'd put his money on Beans, and they competed with stories of canine slothfulness.

How odd that they felt so comfortable with this sweet stranger. Liz pondered how she could possibly fit into Vanessa's ugly schemes.

After Jackson brought them cafeteria coffee, Liz probed gently, "We're so thankful you're doing better. The police said you were quite critical at one time."

"Yes—no thanks to that woman." Mrs. Terrell's mouth pressed into a line. "I thought she wanted to help me. Instead, she intended all along to get rid of me—after she weaseled her way into my will of course. But I doubt that was her main objective. I stood in the way of her grand scheme."

And that was? Liz and Jackson exchanged glances, but didn't ask. Had Vanessa hatched an additional plot to victimize elderly women?

"I've confused you." Sighing, Mrs. Terrell took Liz's hand. "I'm afraid, honey, that there's no way to clarify this except to tell you my whole story."

"We'd love to hear it," Liz assured her, and Jackson nodded assent.

Mrs. Terrell paused, then began, "I was born in the hills of Tennessee, the tenth of twelve children. Our parents could hardly feed us. They drank too much, which made life even harder."

Liz patted her hand, worn to softness.

The lady continued, "I loved school, but saw little chance for education. I decided the only way I could escape that lifestyle was to marry out of it." She fiddled with the bedclothes. "When I was seventeen, I married a smart, sweet boy named Eddie Fuller, who wanted to go to college and be a music teacher. The way he sang—well, it would melt your heart into a puddle." She hugged herself, remembering. "Neither of us graduated from high school, so we worked at low-paying jobs. But we were happy, and we still had our dreams."

With Mrs. Terrell's wistful smile, Liz could easily imagine how beautiful she must have been in her youth.

The smile soon faded. "When I found out I was in a family way, though, I desperately tried to keep it a secret because my boss would have laid me off. Eddie told me to go ahead and quit. He'd work it out." Mrs. Terrell dug fingers into her temple. "The way he worked it out was to take a dangerous job in a sawmill." She closed her eyes, as if still trying to shut out the memory. "Mark was born at home." She gave the date. "Eddie died in an accident at the mill two months later."

Though the woman's loss had occurred decades before, her grief brought tears to Liz's eyes. And that date . . . the same as Liz's father's birthday. And the child had the same name. The room swirled around her.

But even Geoffrey had found out the right name and birth date.

"Mark was beautiful, with big blue eyes. Eddie was so proud of him." Even now, Mrs. Terrell's voice caressed their names. "But after losing my husband, I had to beg my family to take us in. They treated us like dirt. I was determined my precious little boy would not grow up as I had." Her chin dipped to her chest. "It was the hardest thing I've ever done. I went to the county offices and put him up for adoption." Tears poured down the woman's face.

Trembling, Liz dug her nails into her palms. Jackson's hand gripped Liz's shoulder.

"As you've probably guessed, my baby was your daddy, Mark Edward Fuller. He was adopted by a minister and his wife, who changed his last name to theirs: Eckardt."

Liz said nothing. She couldn't.

Despite her lack of response, Mrs. Terrell poured out the rest of her story. "I left home soon after. It took me ten years, but I graduated from college. I married a good man. Though aware of my first marriage, he didn't know about my son. But all those years, I prayed for my baby boy every day. When I lost my husband three years ago, I decided I would find my son, my only child." Her lips quivered. "When I found out he had died, only the fact he had a child consoled me. A little girl. You."

I don't want this. Not now.

Jackson said softly, "Liz cherishes family too, Mrs. Terrell. That's why she moved to Indiana, to find her mother's family. But an impostor, probably connected to Vanessa, recently showed up claiming to be her father's brother."

"I know."

"You know?" Liz's breath escaped and would not return.

"Yes, when your Chief Houghton questioned me yesterday, I told him why I came to Pleasant Creek. That's when he informed me about

Geoffrey Teal, and also about that woman's stealing Mark's song." Her dark eyes snapped. "He thought I should know before I talked to you about . . . this."

Liz said slowly, "Then as my father's relative, you presented an additional obstacle to Vanessa's keeping all the royalties to his song. That's why she wanted to get rid of you."

"Yes. I was so lonely. I fell hook, line, and sinker for her con. I thought she was you." Mrs. Terrell's voice cracked. "I had planned to stay in the area awhile, hoping you and I could get acquainted before I made myself known. But that woman's schemes wrecked everything . . . What am I saying?" She covered her face. "*I* wrecked everything by watching you from a distance, following you around town. The money, the flowers. Foolish attempts at being the grandmother I longed to be."

"You deposited that money?"

She nodded timidly. "Eight thousand dollars. I also sent two bouquets of flowers. I wanted so much to celebrate your wedding with you. But I couldn't even introduce myself, let alone get to know you." She bit her lip. "I was so afraid you'd reject me. After all, I gave your father away. Why should you believe, after all these years, that I care for you?" Fresh tears poured down her lined cheeks.

After Geoffrey, Liz thought she'd closed that door, maybe forever.

Ninety-five percent of her said, *Walk out. Run.*

The other five percent sang in a child's voice, "Over the river and through the woods, to Grandmother's house we go!"

Dry-eyed, Liz said, "Mrs. Terrell, as you can imagine, this is quite a . . . surprise."

"A shock, I'm sure." Wiping her eyes, she lifted her chin. "It is the truth. But if you choose not to believe it, I understand."

The elderly woman was shaking, but that forthright, clear-eyed look stirred something in Liz. That expression—did it resemble her father's in his photo?

Liz hesitated.

Behind her, Jackson laid a hand on her arm.

Liz said, "I was a lawyer, Mrs. Terrell. Especially after this last deception, I can't entertain any thoughts of kinship without absolute proof."

"I understand," she repeated.

"I will, however, pursue that proof as I can." Liz took a deep breath. "And while I reserve the right to stay objective, I won't refuse any reasonable overtures you may extend."

A glow, like the edge of an imminent sunrise, lit Mrs. Terrell's face. "I—I certainly cannot expect more. Thank you." Her voice sank almost to a whisper. "Even if proof of our kinship cannot be found, I will consider knowing you—in any capacity—a treasure worth having."

23

"Okay, what super-useful wedding gift came today?" Sadie asked as she helped Liz lug two boxes inside.

Liz set the smaller box on the rotunda floor. "I thought if we asked wedding guests to support a hunger fund instead of giving presents, that would free me from this. But apparently people insist on donating to charity *and* giving us presents."

"You should be grateful that people *love* you." Sadie gave her a huge, toothy grin.

Liz sighed. "They love us so much that we're now the proud owners of seven framed decoupages of our wedding invitation, eleven first-year-of-marriage Christmas ornaments, and two monogrammed electric ice-cream scoops."

"I can't wait to see what's inside these." Sadie patted the boxes invitingly.

"Yes, open them, dear." Mary Ann had wandered out too.

Liz opened the smaller box. "Looks like a big book. Did somebody buy us a dictionary?"

She unwrapped it and found a family Bible, accented with gold. The card read, *May the Lord bless you both and keep you in His love forever. Pauline Terrell.*

For once, Sadie was speechless.

"Beautiful." Mary Ann said it all in one word.

Liz ran her fingers over the fragrant leather, deeply touched. Pauline had come to coffee hour twice, but she hadn't pressed Liz. So far, they'd gotten along well. Quite well.

Liz had found little time to do additional research on her father's background, but she'd written letters to Tennessee organizations, hoping to receive answers soon.

Jackson breezed in. "Why don't I get to open presents?"

"I'll let you write all the thank-you notes." Liz grinned. She showed him the Bible and card.

"Wow," he murmured. "I'll be glad to write the thank-you for this one."

Liz teased, "Since you are the groom, I suppose you can open the big one."

"That's more like it." He ripped into the second box. "What's this?"

"Yes, what is it?" Liz stared at the pile of black, orange, and purple plastic.

"It's an Ozy!" Jackson's face lit up. "You know, our basketball team's mascot. Our very own Ozy the Owl! And a pump to inflate it!"

Mary Ann, a fanatical basketball fan, clasped her hands. "Put it in the front yard at sectional time! Every year!"

No. Liz had learned to appreciate Hoosier Hysteria almost as much as the next Indiana citizen, but there were limits. "Jackson, you know I decorate the porch every season." *Tastefully.*

"Ozy will be perfect for February and March!"

Liz groaned loudly.

He connected the electric pump, and the plastic pile fattened. The gaudy owl with bared teeth rose, a giant, snarling monster.

"I don't even want to know who gave us that thing." When Jackson regarded her with an almost hurt look, Liz added, "You will definitely write the thank-you for it."

Ozy remained a major topic of conversation that evening when the Girls gathered, supposedly to brainstorm Christmas quilts. They also aimed teasing digs at Liz.

"Who are you going to annoy after I'm an old married lady?" Liz demanded.

"We can start on Caitlyn." Sadie cast a wicked eye at her.

"Don't go there, Sadie," Caitlyn warned. "Liz is nice. I'm not."

"You girls behave," Opal scolded. "Sometimes I feel like I'm teaching second-grade Sunday school again."

Leafing through patterns, Liz chuckled. Every group needed at least one mom. Here in the workroom, Opal and Mary Ann kept the Material Girls in line. Liz's thoughts wandered to her own mother, who had played a similar role in every group she joined.

As much as she loved her substitute mothers, she'd done without her own mom while planning her wedding. Liz's eyes stung. How she hungered to read her mother's diary again, to outline the words with her fingers.

Stan had grilled Vanessa about it. Realizing cooperation might lessen her sentence, she'd confessed more and more details of her crimes. But she continued to insist that Geoffrey, who'd twice burglarized Liz's inn under Vanessa's direction, had refused to give her the diary.

Naomi, sitting next to Liz, touched her arm. "You're quiet. Anything on your mind?"

She told her friend, adding, "Geoffrey might well have destroyed Mom's diary. But it was power—proof that the song was stolen. I wonder if he hid it and planned to double-cross Vanessa with it? Or maybe, as she threatened him more and more, he hid it from her as a kind of insurance."

Insurance that didn't work. Vanessa had confessed that she'd dusted Geoffrey's poppy seed bread with ricin. He'd grown to care for Liz too much and refused to "cooperate."

Cooperate how? By eliminating me? Liz swallowed, glad she didn't have that answer.

"Will you girls focus?" Sadie poked them. "We're talking Christmas quilts here. Holly wreaths, snowmen, and ho ho ho. No long faces tonight."

Naomi said, "First, we should talk about Liz's mother's diary. She's missing her mom."

Hugs definitely helped. So did refreshment time.

Mary Ann carefully sectioned her cinnamon roll into pieces. "So the chief hasn't found any trace of the diary yet?"

"No. But I can't imagine Geoffrey would have destroyed it."

Caitlyn pondered, "If I were a diary, where would I hide? Under beds, in closets, drawers, attics, hollow of trees."

"The construction crew was in our attic. And believe it or not, I've searched the woods not only on my property, but all around the lake." Liz shrugged. "We can't examine every tree in Pleasant Creek. Or poke under every bed."

Opal offered, "Have you searched your library? He might have hidden it among the books."

"Not thoroughly." Opal's suggestion dinged in Liz's mind. "I'll look there again. But I'm remembering something Barb at the bank said. Right before he disappeared, she saw Geoffrey enter the library downtown. Loretta confirmed that he visited the basement."

Mary Ann cocked her head. "Didn't Geoffrey say he hated to read?"

"He did. I would have thought he'd use his smartphone for finding information instead of a strange library." Liz sighed. "No time to search there now. I can look after the wedding."

Opal pursed her lips. "Why not before? We can take turns digging around. Besides, a little organization won't hurt that mess downstairs."

"Not you, Liz." Sadie aimed a finger at her. "You just do wedding stuff."

"Like open more cool presents like Ozy." Caitlyn pouted. "Not that I've seen him yet."

"I haven't either." Naomi pushed back her chair. "Where is Ozy?"

Liz never could remember exactly how the session degenerated. Somehow, the Girls combined planning library duty with dancing around Ozy to the school fight song.

"I'm not even going to ask." Steve dropped in, but quickly fled the scene.

Afterward, enjoying solitude on her bench, Liz wondered if anyone anywhere had friends like the Material Girls—the loving-est, giving-est, weirdest friends in the world.

How differently they partied when Liz invited Jackson's mother.

But Liz didn't mind that Therese's elegant presence civilized their gathering, as she didn't want the Girls to drag out Ozy for the bridesmaids' breakfast.

"We shouldn't call it that," Liz explained to her future mother-in-law, "because I'm having only one bridesmaid, Naomi. But everyone's involved in the wedding. I wanted all my lady friends to come."

"I'm glad you consider me your friend."

Therese's words warmed her. When they'd first met, they'd clashed continually. Liz had feared that Jackson's mother might blame her for his brief incarceration. Instead, they'd had to talk Therese out of siccing high-powered lawyers on the Maypole police.

Though Liz often disagreed with her, they had meshed surprisingly well in planning the wedding. She and Therese were learning to appreciate each other.

"Thank you for inviting me." Pauline, dressed in a pink pantsuit, sported a constant smile.

Ignoring the typical Amish side hug, Miriam threw her arms around Liz. Amid the sisterly hug, she recalled that the bishop never entered English households. Nevertheless, he and Philip had come to the inn to apologize for their mistake.

Welcoming Miriam and Aunt Ruth—who gave her a bear hug—to the breakfast was a gift Liz valued more than she could say.

Kiera Williams filled her with joy as well. Liz's formerly taciturn, poverty-stricken teen employee now exuded confidence with bright hopes for the future. "I can't wait to sing your song," she told Liz, her green eyes sparkling. Liz couldn't wait to hear her.

The Girls, of course, had helped her cook a feast: egg-and-sausage casserole, chocolate croissants, cinnamon-apple scones, and fresh fruit arrangements. Liz had moved the furniture out of the four-season room so they could enjoy the fall sunshine. She set up tables covered with navy tablecloths, her antique blue china, and her best crystal. Pauline had begged to provide bouquets of ivory roses, peach daisies, and greenery. The overall effect was simple and lovely.

After Opal's prayer, they laughed and needled and ate as only women can. Inevitably, the conversation flowed to the past month's ordeal.

Upon hearing Liz's story, Kiera stared, aghast. "Did they ever prove Vanessa killed Geoffrey—I mean, Trey?"

"We call him Geoffrey to avoid confusion." Liz smiled sadly. "Yes, she finally confessed. But only because the police were closing in on her. They found ricin on her clothes and in her hotel room. And they found e-mails and messages in which Vanessa threatened Geoffrey because, in acting like family, he began to want family." Liz shook her head. "He and Vanessa were two of a kind, background-wise. But he wanted to change."

"He really wanted to be Liz's uncle," Mary Ann explained. "Vanessa couldn't allow him to disrupt her plan, which included stealing from multiple musicians."

Liz turned to Pauline. "But the evidence that might interest you is this." She held out her phone.

Pauline stared at the photo. "Old music. It looks handwritten, rather messy."

Liz enlarged the name at the top of the page: Mark Eckardt. "It's the original of 'Love, You Are My Friend.' Vanessa stole it years ago, when they were kids."

Pauline made a small croaking sound.

Nine mouths dropped.

"She was about thirteen. He was seventeen." Liz sighed. "Not only did Dad's adoptive parents take him in, they occasionally cared for foster children. Vanessa, already in trouble with the law, was one of those."

No one spoke.

Liz continued, "She apparently adored my father's music and envied his talent. She probably adored him too. Why else would she have kept the music all these years—especially when it became such damning evidence?" Liz shook her head. "The police found it in her hotel room! Along with several other songs of Dad's that I imagine she meant to exploit too."

"Vanessa kept them in her hotel room?" Opal stared. "That seems unwise."

"She didn't have a home. She failed to make it as an actress, then was jailed for fraud and forgery. After that, her lifelong pattern consisted of prowling around the country, looking for victims."

"What a horrible way to live." Naomi shuddered. "How did you learn all this? You don't have the music, do you?"

"No, it's being held as evidence," Liz said, "but the chief let me take a picture to show you all. As for Vanessa's background, I've been filling in blanks with my own research, plus what the chief and Detective Hawkins have shared. Hawkins and Officer Matthews not only tracked down Eleanor Watson's assistant, they caught Watson too. She's a fellow forger from Vanessa's past. They also found the gun

Watson shot at us in Nashville—because Vanessa threatened her into doing it, she claims."

"I'll bet." Sadie didn't look convinced. "Who called in the bomb threat?"

"Apparently, Watson forced a male employee to call." Liz shook her head. "She's in huge trouble, so she's eager to make a deal and hasn't hesitated to tell all she knows about her old bud."

"I'm glad I had no idea all this was going on." Pauline had paled. "I'm not a brave person."

Liz stood, and for the first time, slipped an arm around her. "I think you're brave. When others lied to me, you told the truth." She dangled two pages before the astonished woman's eyes. "Would you like to read these?"

Pauline first scanned the personal letter, written in a wavering hand on flowery stationery.

"It's from Millie Briggs!" Pauline's hand went to her mouth. "I haven't talked to her in years!"

She devoured the page while Liz whispered to their spellbound audience, "Mildred Briggs was the caseworker who arranged Dad's adoption. She's verified Pauline's story."

Pauline didn't bother to wipe away tears. "Millie was almost a kid herself, but so understanding. What would I have done without her?"

"Mildred didn't retire until she turned seventy, and since then she has remained active as a volunteer." Liz pointed to the other letter, typed on official letterhead. "That's from the head of Child Services, Stacy Tomlinson, vouching for Mildred's former employment dates and her amazing trustworthiness in serving children and their parents. You are my grandmother."

Liz's voice failed her. She held Pauline close as they wept with joy.

When the flood of tears eased to a trickle, Naomi stepped forward with a package wrapped in silver-and-blue paper.

"This may be anticlimactic, Liz," she said, "but we wanted you to have it today."

Liz fumbled with the ribbon. "Help me, will you, Grandma?"

"Certainly, honey." They undid the wrapping, and Liz opened the box inside.

It held her mother's diary.

Liz swayed, and Sadie shoved a chair under her. "Don't you die on us! Not after we went through every shelf and box in that basement."

"Where did you find it?"

"Stuck between *Dr. Scruggs's One Hundred Molasses Cures* and *A Bride's Guide to Hog Butchering.*" Sadie handed Liz both cobwebby books. "We thought you'd find them useful too."

Even Therese fell back in her chair, shrieking with laughter.

Laughing hysterically with her friends, Liz couldn't believe that only a few days before, she'd hit the low point of her life.

Now, holding her mother's diary, with an arm encircling her father's mother, she could only look forward to even better times.

Let the wedding celebration begin!

24

"Every bride has to walk down a stairway," Sadie had insisted. "Otherwise, how will you remember how you swished?"

Liz had humored her, but she didn't really understand until she took her first steps down the rotunda staircase. Her skirt floated like a cloud, the dress's train whispering a wonder-filled *swish.*

All day, the Material Girls had scurried in a hundred different directions. Now, dressed to the nines, they stood below, beaming as Sadie pointed a video camera at Liz.

A person she had never expected to know waited for her on the landing. Pauline, wearing a blue lace dress, welcomed Liz. "Honey, this is even better than my dreams."

"It is, isn't it?" Liz laid her cheek against Pauline's. Then her grandmother lifted her train as Liz glided toward the Girls, arms open.

"You'll wrinkle your dress," Opal cautioned as Liz tried to reach around them all.

"No, the fabric isn't fussy." Laughing, Liz pulled Opal into the group hug. "Even if it was, I wouldn't care. I plan on lots of hugging today."

"Did Jackson and Steve arrive at the church on time to dress?" Mary Ann was still checking lists.

Liz laughed. "Therese made it her business to get them there early."

"We want you there early too." Mary Ann gestured. "Sadie, go get the van."

Liz would have loved to ride with all the Girls, but the Sew Welcome partners had removed back seats so she and her dress could fit. It wasn't a limousine, but it was roomy. Sadie chauffeured and Naomi, wearing a filmy peach dress and tiny ivory flowers worked into her dark hair, rode beside Liz while the others took Pauline to the church.

Waning September also had donned its best end-of-summer dress for the occasion.

"Just for you and Jackson." Naomi exulted in nature's beauty.

Yes. For us. After weeks of misery, today's sunshine gleamed all the brighter.

"The outdoor pictures by the lake and gazebo should be wonderful," Naomi said.

"We hope so." They'd had the main photos taken beforehand. "I usually feel awkward posing in front of photographers. But Sadie made it fun."

Their irrepressible friend had worn her purple pom-pom hat to the session. Now she whined, "I wanted to wear that hat to the wedding. But you know Mary Ann."

Liz and Naomi giggled like teenagers, but Liz privately thanked God for Mary Ann's sane influence.

"I can't quite believe the wedding's going to happen."

"You'd better." Naomi grinned at her. "Do you know how hard it is to run a bakery and still fit into this dress?"

They bantered and laughed until Sadie guided the van to the church's back door. Once inside, Mary Ann rushed them to the room that served as a freshening-up station. Caitlyn, sleek and stylish in navy satin, reexamined her earlier work, touching up Liz's hair and makeup in a large oval mirror she'd brought. Opal wore a soft, lilac-colored suit. Mary Ann and Sadie, who were to precede Liz down the aisle, wore dresses in a similar light-blue palette. Mary Ann wore a classic light-blue A-line featuring a long, filmy scarf wrapped around her slim throat, the ends floating behind her like angel wings. Sadie sported layers of large ruffles and an asymmetrical hemline that made her resemble an elegant flapper. She'd crocheted the ivory flower pinned onto her elegant hat.

They all wore the brooches Liz had given them that summer, and they all looked perfect. When Liz said as much, the Girls argued, "No, you do."

"Look in the mirror!"

"You're a vision!"

Delicate ivory flowers softened the French braid framing her face, and the rest of her shining hair fell to her shoulders. Her skin had taken on a peaches-and-cream glow, enhanced by a minimal amount of makeup. Jackson's gift, the pearl-studded locket, glimmered at her throat, and the dress—oh, the dress! No fairy-tale princess had ever felt more magical.

Naomi handed Liz her simple bouquet. The ivory and pale-peach roses, accented with a few coral lilies, tiny waxflowers, and ivy, filled the room with their fragrance.

Naomi arranged the bouquet's navy and ivory ribbons just so. She glanced at a wall clock. "Fifteen minutes. We'd better take our places."

"Just a second." Liz held up a hand. She met each Material Girl's gaze. "I just want to say I love you all."

Murmurs of "We love you too" wrapped around her as Liz—Naomi lifting her train—walked into the wide hallway. Acoustic guitar music drifted from the sanctuary's back entrance. How fortunate that Caitlyn had musical friends.

"Ready, Mom?" Steve, who had appeared right on cue, wore a beautifully tailored charcoal-gray suit that he had bought in Fort Wayne and that Sadie had altered to fit him perfectly. He offered her his arm and grinned. "You made a good choice," he said. "Jackson is a great guy."

Liz smiled up at her son. "And so are you. I love you, Steve."

"I love you too, Mom. Now let's go."

When they reached the open double doors of the sanctuary, Liz steeled herself. Most of the town filled the pews.

Juan Fernandez, Jackson's childhood friend who had already seated Pauline and Therese, now escorted Opal to a front seat, as she would be reading the Bible passage they had chosen. Caitlyn disappeared momentarily and returned with Beans. He wore a fancy navy coat and an enormous ivory satin bow tie. A matching satin pillow with both wedding rings had been strapped to his back.

"Beans, baby!" Sadie squealed. "You look so dashing!"

Liz raised a sincere prayer that the bulldog wouldn't fall asleep halfway down the aisle, as he had at rehearsal.

Fortunately, she had little time to worry about it. Juan returned to escort Mary Ann and Sadie to their seats of honor in the front row, next to her newly found grandmother. The guitar music ended, and two violins and a cello began Pachelbel's "Canon in D." Caitlyn, holding Beans's satin leash, took her place at the door with Naomi behind her, carrying a basket of rose petals.

As she and Steve stood in the door, pausing before making their entrance, Liz saw Jackson standing tall and handsome at the altar. His eyes sparkled, and her heart skipped a bit when his gaze met hers.

Beans made a hit with the congregation as he waddled alongside Caitlyn toward the altar. Then he promptly dropped for a nap at Jackson's feet.

Naomi gracefully walked along the tulle-lined aisle.

Steve looked at her as if asking her permission, and she nodded to her son. She was ready. They made their way to the front, where Jackson and Stan Houghton, Jackson's best man, waited with Pastor Brad.

How she loved Jackson's hand holding hers, his strong voice vowing his love to her forever, his earnest face as they approached the large, ivory unity candle, surrounded by peach roses and greenery.

Earlier, Therese had set a picture of Jackson as a boy, shown with his late father, by his candle. Liz had set her mother's picture and diary by her candle. Behind the unity candle, a large, framed copy of her father's manuscript had been placed on a stand. In front of the candle, Liz had opened their new family Bible to Genesis 2.

Now, as they lit their individual candles, Opal read sacred words: "And the Lord God said, 'It is not good that man should be alone; I will make him a helper comparable to him.'" She continued with Song of Solomon 8:7: "Many waters cannot quench love; nor can the floods drown it. If a man would give for love all the wealth of his house, it would be utterly despised."

Then, as they lit the unity candle, Kiera sang in her clear, sweet voice. Liz reveled in Jackson's gaze as Kiera sang the last verse:

I've stopped running from love. You're the rose that lasts,

I've stopped running from love, stronger than my past.

You are the love Love sent to me

To help set me free

To take me home

Make me your own forever,

Love, you are my friend.

Love, you are my friend.

Afterward, Pastor Brad's joyful prayer of thanksgiving nearly moved Liz to tears. God had blessed them beyond measure.

Then the pastor pronounced them husband and wife.

Jackson, eyes aglow like the candles, sought her lips in their first tender, married kiss. Pastor, attendants, and congregation vanished as Liz melted into his arms.

The sanctuary erupted in applause and cheers that startled them and woke a disgruntled Beans. But Liz and Jackson fairly skipped down the aisle to the exit, where he said, "I told you nothing would keep us from happily ever after."

The Material Girls left immediately afterward to prepare for guests at the inn. Liz and Jackson, with Steve, Pauline, and Therese, hugged a thousand people, it seemed. After a few brief church photos taken by the photographer they'd hired, they exited the church.

It was so good to be outside in the sunshine. She caught Jackson's eye. Scratch that. It was even better to be married.

Horses' whinnies in the parking lot reminded Liz that she'd asked Miriam and Philip to drive them to the reception. She'd known better than to ask them to the ceremony. But their bishop would allow her cousins to attend the meal afterward.

When they reached the parking lot, however, a dozen buggies waited, including those of Sarah and her husband, Isaac, as well as Aunt Ruth, Uncle Amos—and even the bishop's!

Miriam contained her emotions, but her smile said it all as she squeezed Liz's hand.

So Liz and Jackson savored the mellow September day as the buggy convoy carried them to the inn. They arrived at the inn, where Steve and Naomi led them to the backyard. Pastor Brad blessed the meal, and all served themselves from blue-covered tables groaning with food.

"Ohhhhh!" Liz had seen the decorations during their earlier photo session. But at the head of the eating area, someone had placed a beautifully crafted arbor, covered with fresh flowers, under which stood a table for two. Only when Liz examined them closely did she realize the rich wood and carvings of the two pieces matched.

She turned to Jackson and Steve, who wore twin smiles. "You made these, didn't you?"

"Guilty as charged," Steve said.

Sadie took pictures while Jackson showed her where shelves could be inserted into the sturdy arbor. "I hope we can place these pieces somewhere in the inn to remind us of today."

"Oh, we'll find a place." She threw her arms around him, then Steve. "Thank you. What a precious gift."

Some guests had gathered near to watch, but soon the rest discovered their presence. Loud cheers and applause echoed across the inn's grounds.

Liz and Jackson waved and smiled, but Liz murmured, "Aren't there at least three times as many people as we invited?" *What if we run out of food?*

"Don't worry." Jackson winked. "Mary Ann has everything in hand."

She eyed him. "Was this a conspiracy?"

"Of course. She enlisted the entire Amish community to empty their pie safes."

So Mary Ann *had* masterminded the gala of the year, despite Liz's efforts to keep the reception under control. Liz chuckled and clicked her tongue. "She just can't help it."

The incurable party girl herself was carrying a big blue-and-silver box toward them, trailed by the other Material Girls, Miriam, and

Aunt Ruth. They clumped together as Mary Ann set it on their new table. "For both of you. With our love."

"But you already made our wedding quilt," Liz protested.

"We made you *a* quilt." Mary Ann had assumed a look of abject surprise. "But we never called it your wedding quilt, did we, girls?"

"Oh, no."

"Goodness, no."

They all grinned like pleased cats.

As Jackson and Liz—Liz trying not to sniffle—opened the box and pushed aside tissue, Mary Ann pointed. "*This* is your wedding quilt."

Liz gasped, then caressed a cream-colored, scallop-edged masterpiece, with exquisite double wedding ring and floral designs etched into it by thousands of tiny, exact hand stitches. It was an heirloom to be treasured for generations.

"It—it's beautiful." Liz clung to them.

"Thank you all." Even Jackson's voice cracked.

Stroking the exquisite needlework, Liz said, "When did you do this? Wouldn't this quilt take months and months to finish?"

"We started it almost two years ago," Naomi informed her.

"Two years? But we've only been engaged since May!"

Now their faces could hardly contain their catty smiles. Mary Ann said smugly, "You both were slow about getting together, but we knew you'd finally get around to it."

Their laughter was drowned out by motorcycles roaring into Liz's backyard.

Big Berky Parker—a biker Liz had helped clear of murder charges—strode up, kissed Liz's cheek, and pumped Jackson's hand. His biker friends—Scooby, Pixie, Bulldog, and Shine—soon followed.

Their greeting set a pattern for the next hour. Kiera had invited Asher Hilty, an ex-Amish basketball player, whom Liz also had proved innocent of the murder of the town's basketball coach. The coach's daughter, Corinne, who had also been a suspect, wished them a wonderful life together. Lori Tatum, wearing a camo outfit that somehow became her, introduced her new boyfriend, Les—also clad in camo.

"A match made in a heavenly deer stand," Jackson whispered as the couple joined other diners.

Beaming Vera and Violet Holmes, elderly sisters who had visited the inn numerous times, clasped their hands and congratulated them. Violet recently had married Stefan Meyer, who occasionally served as the inn's handyman. The two sets of newlyweds shared their mutual joy.

Two delightful occasional guests who topped the "most unique" list, also came. Midge and Wilbur Rockwell, gravestone historians, threw their arms around Liz and Jackson.

"We're giving you two a special wedding gift." Midge's blue eyes sparkled.

"One that will last forever," Wilbur added.

They chorused, "Side-by-side cemetery plots!"

Fortunately, the Rockwells loved food almost as much as they loved all things moribund, so Liz and Jackson didn't immediately have to take them up on their offer for free gravestone consultations.

After greeting numerous Boston friends too, Liz finally sat at her lovely handcrafted table. Naomi and Steve brought them full plates and glasses.

"Sorry you couldn't choose your food," Naomi said, "but we were afraid you'd never make it to the serving tables."

After a quick meal, they went to the lighted gazebo, where Naomi's enormous, elegant wedding cake, with its fresh peach roses and greenery inspired unanimous "oohs" and "aahs."

What if I knock it over? With coaching from Naomi and Jackson's steady hand over hers, though, Liz cut the first pieces without incident.

While Kiera again sang, "Love, You Are My Friend," they danced in the gazebo, gazes locked together as if in a world of their own. The first stars peered from behind twilight curtains, and an orange harvest moon glowed approval from the lake horizon.

The DJ took over, and other couples joined them in the gazebo and on the temporary dance floor surrounding it. It was like a scene from a fairy tale, the twinkly lights overhead casting an enchanting glow on the dancers in their finery. Miriam gave Liz a quick goodbye hug, and she and her family joined most of the Amish guests, who headed for their buggies—but not before treating the guests to a few songs featuring their unique Swiss yodeling, which concluded with a rousing round of applause.

Soon more music swept Liz back into Jackson's arms and onto the dance floor. Caitlyn and Steve whirled past. Did the glow in their faces hint at a budding relationship? While harboring a secret smile, Liz gave thanks for Caitlyn's care that had sped his recovery.

Liz spotted Naomi in the arms of Evan, a quirky young man she'd met at a baker's conference. Sadie was dancing with Mr. Cyrus Whittington, a millionaire Liz had helped rescue from a greedy relative. Debonair as ever, Mr. Whittington wore his usual top hat, a red-and-white-striped tuxedo jacket with green pants, and neon orange tennis shoes. The couple waved as they spun past Liz and Jackson.

"Old guy really did himself proud tonight," Jackson whispered.

They danced and chatted with their guests, and danced and chatted some more. Fun, but when Jackson murmured into her ear, "You want to leave?" Liz replied, "I thought you'd never ask."

Quickly, he signaled Mary Ann, who announced the tossing of the bouquet.

A sea of single women gathered below the gazebo. Liz turned and threw the bouquet over her shoulder. At the laughter and catcalls that followed, she turned to see Caitlyn, face as red as her hair, holding the bouquet.

"I told you Caitlyn's next!" Sadie crowed at Steve.

Steve didn't seem to mind the implication.

Liz and Jackson hurried to change, hoping to slip away. As they descended the rotunda stairs, however, a mariachi band greeted them, their boisterous music echoing off the walls.

"Juan's family wanted to give you a send-off," Mary Ann informed them. "I hope you don't mind."

"Of course not. Juan's an old friend. And we've had yodeling, why not a mariachi band?"

But not before Liz spotted Juan's huge family carrying more covered dishes, baskets, and coolers toward her backyard.

"Homemade Mexican food for everybody!" Juan called, and most of the crowd cheered. The mariachi band, playing its loudest number yet, brought up the rear.

When Jackson thanked him for the surprise, Juan smiled. "Thought the food might keep them from following you."

Only a dozen cars tagged after Jackson's speeding, decorated truck, honking through downtown.

However, Steve and Caitlyn, who had covered her telltale hair with a scarf, drove the decoy while Jackson and Liz sneaked to the Acura, loaded with baggage and parked in a nearby alley.

He floored it, and they escaped to the country.

Within an hour, they pulled into the driveway of a cottage overlooking Moon Lake. Electric candles shone in its windows so Liz could see its native rock construction. Lanterns on the circular stone porch illuminated the autumn wreath on the door and the pumpkins and mums decorating the entry.

"Jackson, it's gorgeous." She felt herself relaxing already.

"Want to unwind before we go in?" Jackson gestured. "I happen to know there's a very nice bench down by the water."

He took a warm blanket, a paper bag, and a thermos from the car. "Hot cider and muffins. Funny how people don't get to eat much at their own weddings."

They held hands in the now-silver light, watching the moon paint its colors on the lake's waves. Jackson told her he'd reserved the cottage for two days, then booked a two-week trip to Orcas Island, Washington, between Seattle and Vancouver.

"Sounds incredible." She'd never explored the Pacific Northwest.

"But for now, we just need some serious loafing time." He pulled out his phone and turned it off. "No more phones. No more mysteries. Can you do that?"

He squeezed her hand and she felt contentment like she'd never known wash over her. She sent up a silent thank-you to her mother for bringing her to Pleasant Creek, where she now had everything she needed or wanted. Friends. Family. And Jackson.

"You didn't answer my question," he teased.

"I've already promised to love, honor, and cherish you today. Isn't that enough?" Liz smiled up at her new husband. She couldn't help it if more mysteries found her down the road.

He smiled back at her, as if reading her thoughts. "That's the only promise I'll ever need."

Learn more about Annie's fiction books at

AnniesFiction.com

We've designed the Annie's Fiction website especially for you!

Access your e-books • Read sample chapters • Manage your account

Choose from one of these great series:

Amish Inn Mysteries
Annie's Attic Mysteries
Annie's Mysteries Unraveled
Annie's Quilted Mysteries
Annie's Secrets of the Quilt
Antique Shop Mysteries
Chocolate Shoppe Mysteries
Creative Woman Mysteries
Hearts of Amish Country
Secrets of the Castleton Manor Library
Victorian Mansion Flower Shop Mysteries

What are you waiting for? Visit us now at **AnniesFiction.com!**